# *Barnburner*

*by*

*Sharon Lee*

SRM Publisher Ltd.
PO Box 179
Unity Maine 04988

Barnburner Copyright © 2002 by Sharon Lee

First electronic edition April 2002, Embiid Publishing

ISBN: 0-9722473-0-0

Cover design by Steve Miller

First SRM Publisher Ltd. edition, July 2002

Printed in the United States of America

0 9 8 7 6 5 4 3 2 1

# *Barnburner*

## *by*

## *Sharon Lee*

**SRM Publisher Ltd.**
**PO Box 179**
**Unity Maine 04988**

*Any errors in this book are, of course, my own. However, special thanks are due:*

*To Peter Stowell, who knew the words.*
*To Lou McIntosh, who'd been a cop.*
*To eluki bes shahar, who wanted to see the rest.*
*To Mary Grow, for her eagle eye.*
*To all the users of Circular Logic BBS and Maine Meeting Place BBS, for being there.*
*And to my husband, Steve Miller. He knows why.*

*— Sharon Lee*

*Note:*
*There is no Wimsy, Maine.*
*The Big Smoke River is a figment.*
*The Waterville and Wimsy Railroad never was.*
*Likewise, the Electric Track Division.*
*In short, this is a work of fiction.*
*Any resemblance to non-fictional people,*
*dead or alive, is just a lucky guess.*
*— SL*

9

# 1989

# Central Maine

# 1

THE PICKUP TRUCK HAD been blue once, but general neglect and six winters of road salt had scrubbed it down to gray. It was lacy with rust around the wheel wells— salt again— and clanged like a sheet metal convention the long way down the drive and into the dooryard.

I rinsed out the coffee mug and put it to drain, pulled the plug in the kitchen sink and wiped my hands down the seat of my jeans.

"Harry's here," I told Jasper, a banality he vanquished with a single flick of his right ear. Jasper's ears are very expressive. Mostly they express Jasper's irritation with his present body servant. Jasper had been quite happy with his former servant, my Aunt Jennifer, and had been inclined from the first to lay blame for her sudden and unexplained desertion squarely at my door.

I inclined my head as I passed him in his window-perch—"Your Majesty"— worked the latch on the ancient plank door and stepped out onto the porch.

Harry was standing on the truck's risky back bumper, bent over the gate and swearing so matter-of-factly that she might have been holding a Sunday social conversation with the rusty bedboards.

"Gotcha!" she announced as I came down the porch steps.

Awkwardly, she gathered a brown paper shopping bag into her arms and came upright, swaying with a certain Chaplin-esque precarity before simply stepping backward off the bumper.

I stretched my legs. Harry hit the ground, tottered— and grinned up at me as I grabbed her shoulders.

"Damn good thing you happened by. I'd've bruised my ass."

I laughed. "What's in the bag?"

"Beans," Harry said, with relish. She headed for the porch, bag cradled against her chest.

"Beans," I repeated, eyeing the bag with misgiving.

"Cull beans," Harry expanded, setting the bag on the top step and treating me to another grin. "Least, it's what they said down to the company. Bought a sackful for the sheep, opened her up just now— damn beans are just about perfect. Thought you could use some, with winter coming."

The Maine year is measured by winter— it's either coming, just gone, or here. In this case, Harry's point was made with a Mainer's understatement: it was mid-October, and winter breathing down our necks.

"Brought twenty pound, thereabout," Harry said, pulling her flannel shirt straight. "Go on and bring out some bowls. I'll sit an hour and help you pick 'em."

Twenty pounds of beans, I thought, dismally. What on earth was I going to do with twenty pounds of beans?

It was impossible not to take the beans, just as it was impossible to decline the offered assistance. *Manners, Jen*, I told myself severely and started into the house.

"Glass of cider?" I asked Harry, holding the door open on my fingertips.

"That'd be fine."

Haroldene Pelletier was Jennifer Pierce's oldest friend and I had inherited her, with the house and Jasper, when Aunt Jen died, two years ago. She was a stocky, gap-toothed woman with shoulder-length gray hair squeezed flat under a succession of well-used peaked caps. Today's hat was blue, with a faded GMC logo over the bill. It looked about as old as the usetabe-blue pickup.

I handed Harry a beer mug filled with cider and sat down on the step, the bag of beans between us. I waited until she'd had a sip before handing her the largest of Aunt Jen's nesting pottery bowls.

"Good cider," she said, setting the mug down with a thump.

"Morris brought it by yesterday."

"Morris" is Mainer for Maurice. This particular Maurice is DuChamp, owner of Old Smoky Orchard, and, as far as I knew, the last of my aunt's living bequests.

"Well, we've had our differences," Harry said, which was her standard Morris line, "but I will say Morris DuChamp knows how to behave."

She unrolled the top of the bag and reached in, pulling out a fistful of beans. She opened her fingers and showed me: pale beans with a scattering of faded red freckles along the seam, liberally mixed with stones, sticks, bits of hay, and beans that were nowhere near "perfect."

I set the enameled colander one step down, hooked a leg up, planted the opposite foot two steps down ("High pockets," Harry said, the first time we met. "Just like your aunt."), and nestled the second-largest bowl in the crook of my knee.

"What kind of beans are these?" I asked, gamely reaching into the bag and hauling out a fistful.

"Soldier," Harry said, head bent over her hand. "You got a good recipe for baked beans in your aunt's card tin—'Thena Gagnon copied it out for her. Bean pot used to be in the bottom of the hutch."

At first, it had frosted me utterly that these people—

these *strangers*— knew more about the contents and keepings
of my home than I did. Now and then I still had the urge to
move everything in the house completely around and then
hold a potluck for the neighbors. It was only the bone-deep
belief that the neighbors would work day and night to put
everything back "right" that saved the house and Jasper from
disruption.

I opened my fist and began to sort. Sticks, stones and
icky wrinkly, dried-up once-beans were the easy discards.
They clattered into the colander like sudden hail.

Now, for the harder choices. I chose a pristine, plump
specimen from the pile in my palm and dropped it into my
bowl. Another... another.

The next one was slightly wrinkled. I consider it;
flicked it into the colander.

"You be at the meeting tonight?"

I sighed down at my little clutch of beans.

"It was on my sheet yesterday," I said, sounding almost
as grumpy as I felt. "I guess it'll be on my sheet today." I
discarded a cracked bean and a wrinkled one and hesitated
over a pea-sized specimen before dropping it into the bowl.

"I wish Reverend Stern would get a life," I grumbled.

Harry sniffed. "Always poking his nose into other
people's houses," she said, sorting beans with efficient flicks of
her finger. Her bowl was filling rapidly; the discards to the
colander alarmingly few. "That way in elementary school. No
use looking for him to change now."

"Maybe he'll move away," I suggested.

Harry raised wide eyes to my face. "Whatever for?"

I grinned, sourly. "Yeah, why move to a city and be
just another crank when you can be a big fool in a little
town?"

Harry gave a crack of laughter. "Boss fish eats better

than the minnows," she commented and shook her head. "Where does that man get his money?"

"He goes to Boston once a month and robs a bank."

"Wouldn't think he was bold as that."

I hiccuped against a laugh and threw Harry a grin. "You're probably right."

"Not as if they didn't come asking for notice," Harry said, reaching into the bag for another fistful of beans. "*He's* quiet enough, but *her*— she might as well have popped the Reverend in the nose and had done with it."

*Him* and *her* were Scott and Merry Ash, who'd bought the old Johnson place at the top of the Point Road. They'd moved in at the end of mud season— which is called April in most of the rest of the country— and started fixing the place up: roof, shingles, dooryard steps. They'd cleared the rubbish out of the abandoned kitchen garden and put in a modest planting, to the general approval of the neighborhood.

Scott acquitted himself well under interrogation by the old men who held morning court at Christie's Donuts. He had admitted to planning for a sheep or two, an herb garden for Merry, setting in more vegetables, maybe starting a hive.

*Nice young couple,* the preliminary verdict went out from the donut court. *Want to do right by the land.*

Then Merry hit town.

In this age of Christian fundamentalism, Merry Ash is a Witch or— her preference— a Wiccan. Which is to say, a person embracing a specifically non-Christian— some insist, pre-Christian— belief system. Wicca honors a Goddess and a God, and a Wiccan keeping to the letter of her Rede honestly strives to "harm none."

Wimsy is home to half-a-dozen assorted pagans that I know of, and probably twice that many who prefer to keep their beliefs quite, quite secret. What set Merry and Scott apart was that neither of them attempted to hide their affiliation. Indeed, Merry set out to educate others about her beliefs, and quickly became one of the more popular— and controversial— speakers at the local schools.

But trouble, when it sprang, didn't spring from a Wiccan-versus-Christian matter at all.

It exploded out of the abortion debate.

Reverend Stern was pro-life, militantly so. He picketed the Wimsy Medical Center, there being no "abortionaries" on this side of the Smoke. He'd had a heart attack in February which had kept him close to home all summer, but before that he'd traveled extensively throughout Maine and the rest of the continental forty-eight, to the relief of the greater portion of Wimsy's townsfolk, organizing rallies at other hospitals, medical centers and clinics.

In June, he'd taken his fervor to the streets, organizing a couple dozen staunch supporters to march as a bloc in the annual We Are Wimsy Day Parade.

So, picture it: Reverend Stern and his followers, with their placards of graphically ravaged fetuses, jostling through the crowd to find their place in the parade queue— and coming face-to-placard with Merry Ash and the founding membership of Gaia Coven.

The *Wimsy Voice* had been there, which meant me and Dan Skat. Dan won *Best Grab* from the Mid-Maine Newspaper Association for the shot of Merry wrenching Reverend Stern's placard out of his hands.

Merry was ticketed by Officer Vince Kellor and had to pay a fine for littering. After she beat the placard to death against the side of the post office she left the pieces scattered around the parking lot.

If she'd thrown the bits into the rubbish bin, Vince told the *Voice*, he'd have had no cause to write any tickets.

Far as he knew, there wasn't no law against busting placards. As for the placard in question having belonged to Reverend Stern before its demise— "The gentleman was not able to prove ownership."

"You know," Harry commented, dry-voiced. "I bet some of them beans'll cook up just as good as those pretty ones you're keeping."

I started, recalled to the present, and looked up guiltily. "Too picky, huh?"

Harry sighed. "I don't know how them folks in the city get on."

"Too picky," I concluded, and felt a sweep of nostalgia for the bright, wide-aisled supermarkets of *my* hometown.

Gamely, I reached into the bag again, deliberately chose a wrinkled bean and dropped it into my bowl.

"Bad enough they write letters back and forth to each other, clogging up the whole newspaper," Harry continued, back with Scott and Merry and Reverend Stern. "But when he comes knocking on doors and quoting Scripture at me during my supper-hour— " She shook her head, and hauled another fistful of beans out of the bag.

The letter-writing war had been closely followed by all of Wimsy. Merry, at least, stuck to the abortion issue, and if she did from time to time cite her authority as a Wiccan High Priestess, it was no less than Reverend Stern did, by claiming a first-name relationship with Jesus.

But the Reverend just couldn't leave well enough alone. Merry looked like getting the best of him in the abortion debate, to judge by the letters that poured through the *Voice's* editorial desk, and he'd veered off into "Thou shalt not suffer a Witch" territory.

This had proved to be an unexpectedly fruitful field and the Reverend had tilled it and tended it with the devotion of a fanatic all the long, letter-writing summer.

But even that fertile territory had started to dry up after awhile. Folks started to write less fevered, more normal letters to the editor; Gaia Coven opened a co-op on Main Street; those who did went upcountry, late summer, and raked blueberries for their winter's cash. The staff of the *Wimsy Voice* breathed a cautious sigh of relief.

Then Scott applied for the town's permission to fix his barn.

Since there were significant portions of former barn still standing, this should have been a formality. Scott went to Town Hall on Thursday, filled out the form and paid his three dollar fee. Friday morning, the clerk posted his request and two others like it on the public notice board. There it was destined to remain until the next Friday, by which time anyone with objections should have come forward and said their piece.

Reverend Stern didn't stop with saying his piece to the Wimsy Town Clerk. No sir. Reverend Stern took to the streets, to the churches and, yes, once again to the letters page of the *Voice.*

"Calling a whole meeting over a barn," Harry grumbled, sorting beans like a dervish. "Think even Butchie Stern'd have more sense than that."

I choked. *"Butchie?"*

She looked at me from under her lashes, sidewise-sly. "What we called him in elementary school."

"I love it."

"Don't you go using that in no story," Harry admonished. "Have him after *me* in the editorials."

She flicked the last bean from her palm to her bowl and rubbed her hands down faded denim thighs.

"Time to be getting on," she said, putting the bowl up.

"This here's enough to get you started."

She swigged the dregs of her cider and stood. "You look up that recipe, now, and let me know how you like them beans."

"I'll do that," I said, unwinding from the step and walking with her toward the faded blue truck. I smiled as she hauled herself into the driver's seat. "Thanks, Harry."

"You betcha. See you at meeting."

I blinked in surprise. "You're going?"

"Wouldn't miss that show for the world," she said and started the truck with a roar.

# 2

WIMSY IS LOCATED IN Central Maine, which stretches, more or less, from Rockland, across to Kingfield, down to Lewiston and up to Bangor.

Some will say Kingfield, that's *western*. Others will say Rockland's *coast*. But, more or less, with a couple hundred miles swapped around to keep the neighbors civil, that's Central Maine.

Maine has its share of odd town names— Robinhood, China, Norridgewock, Ducktrap— and there's nothing all that odd about Wimsy, once you know it was called after Jebediah Wimsy, who settled the Point along about 1780.

Barges came up the Smoke from Hallowell, which was a seaport, those days, took on Jeb Wimsy's board and left him sugar, cattle and tools. In time, the farming sawmill became a settlement; the settlement became a town.

A hundred Maine towns were made the same way: the place where someone stopped for the wood, or the ice; the place where the horse died. The place beyond which someone could not walk another step.

Waterville is the nearest city, two miles from Wimsy Main Street, across the Big Smoke River. Next town beyond that is Winslow, across two more rivers— Sebasticook and Kennebec. Three or four miles south, where the Smoke gets swallowed by the Kennebec, is Twin Rivers State Park, right at the Vassalboro town line.

There are four ways from Wimsy to Waterville: bang across the Smoke by boat— snowmobile, in winter— by foot, across the Penny Tollbridge; by car— or by Division.

"Goddamned *his*-tor-ical *land*mark!" The big voice

smacked me in the ears as I rounded the corner into the newsroom hall.

*Oh, God,* I thought, closing my eyes. *Is it that time of the year already?*

"...breach of the goddamned *contract*," the voice continued and I opened my eyes, lip-synching the rest of the tirade as I continued down the hall. "By Jesus, I'll see their ass in *court!*"

I stepped into the newsroom.

The only large thing about Norbert Lyons *is* his voice, which I guess is fortunate for us all. Small, spare and demented, he leaned over the half-wall, elbow braced on Bill Jacques' monitor, one finger leveled at Bill's nose.

"Okay, Colonel." Bill's face was red and he leaned back in his chair, keeping well away from that jabbing finger.

"Okay, Colonel," the little man shouted. "You damned scandalmongers don't care what happens to this town's heritage! Least you could do is print a story— "

"We did," I said. Colonel Lyons jerked back and turned his head to glare up at me.

"Did what?" He did not add *flatlander,* but his tone made it plain.

"Did write a story," I told him, with the mindless, neutral patience every secretary worth a keyboard learns early in her career. "Two stories. Last year about this time. You were going to kick Waterville's butt. Make them lay new track along Water Street. The City Administrator talked to your lawyer. You and your lawyer went to a couple council meetings and it got tabled." That was probably enough, but my bad angel prodded me in the larynx and I added:

"Just like it has for the past seven years."

He straightened up real fast and set both fists on his hips.

"So I'm an old fool, am I, *Miz* Pierce? That's what's wrong with you flatlanders— no sense of what's history. In Maine, we got history and the Waterville and Wimsy Railroad's Electric Track Division is it!"

He held out one hand, hard palm pushing air at me. "Well, you and the Waterville Goddamn City Council can sit on your asses and smirk. And keep on smirking while Sawyer Wells drags the goddamn mayor and the goddamn city administrator and the whole goddamn *council* to court and makes them honor what's written down in black and white!" He nodded once, hard, turned on his heel and stamped out of the newsroom.

"So there," Bill muttered and looked up at me with a crooked, red-faced grin.

I grinned back. "Who's Sawyer Wells? The messiah?"

"Close enough." He pulled in tight to his computer and shook his head. "Hotshot lawyer out of Portland, charging Boston fees and working on his legend."

"Wow. And Colonel Lyons is up to that?"

"Maybe he won the lottery," Bill said and started to hit keys.

I turned toward my desk, third in a line of three set against the hall wall. Bill looked up.

"You're on the barn story?"

"Who else?"

He shrugged: editorial impatience with reportorial bitching. "How many inches?"

"How the hell do I know? Harry Pelletier says the whole town's going to be there. Might have to move it out to Turner's field and charge admission."

"Good way to supplement taxes." He reached across to

his desk and pawed at a stack of sheets— the blank pages of tomorrow's newspaper. "I'll save you five on page one."

*"Five?"*

He gave me a sideways, evil-eyed grin. "So it jumps. You got a problem?"

"No suh, boss." I headed for my desk.

***

THE *WIMSY VOICE* is published three times a week: Monday, Wednesday and Friday. The publishers, John and Jerry Talbot, live in sunny Phoenix, Arizona, and make three or four lightning trips to Maine every year, usually during the summer. They acquired the newspaper from Barbara and Tilden Rancourt, who had never been further south than Portland until they retired, sold the paper and moved to Miami on the proceeds.

It being October, we were now officially safe from the twins for a solid eight months and Bill Jacques would run things with dour efficiency, in between complaining about how the twins were sucking the paper to dust. The Winter Shift, Dan Skat called it, around a huge, mimed yawn.

I reached behind the bulky, old-fashioned terminal and snapped the switch up, listening to the computer grumble as it fired up the awesome computing power of a full ten megabyte hard drive. The screen flickered, then steadied. The amber letters were grainy, listing a little to the right.

*Karen's Computer* read the legend at the top of the four-choice menu.

Karen Hopkins had been third-desk reporter before me. She'd fled back to her native California at the end of her second Maine autumn, unable to face another Winter Shift. Desk and computer had been mine for eighteen months, but I'd never gotten around to changing the name on the menu.

I keyed in "1," for "Write" and reached for my notes while Karen's Computer gulped and stammered and finally presented a wavery processing screen.

I flipped through my pad, frowning at the jumble of half-English and shorthand that was my own special note-taking cryptography. A week ago, one Justin Veilleux, 15, had apparently taken his mother's new Escort down to the abandoned quarry at the end of the Stone Road and tried to see what she could do.

According to the skid-mark experts, she'd been doing about seventy when Justin lost his nerve and hit the brakes. God and gravity knew what she was doing just before she smashed into the jagged stone bottom of the main dig. Suffice to say that she had enough speed on her to handily finish off both Justin and the car.

Yesterday, Wimsy High School had held a Remember Justin gathering, where all the kids in the tenth grade came together and talked about Justin and how they felt about his death. The *Voice,* meaning Jen Pierce, had been there.

Sighing, I squared off in front of Karen's Computer, closed my eyes for a second and began to type.

For the record, in case there is one, I am not a reporter by trade. As a matter of fact, I'm not *anything* by trade, as a quick glance at my resume will reveal.

I'd done my time in a steno pool at the small county college where I earned my forty or so undergrad credits; got promoted to department secretary. Took a side job setting type for a weekly paper, when setting type was an IBM Selectric with a special tape drive rigged into its guts. Left the college for an ad agency, where I went from receptionist to

junior copy writer in a meteoric three-year rise. When the
firm was sold I freelanced PR and ad copy, sold computers,
did some waitressing, worked temp when the balance
dipped too low in the checkbook, and finally went back to
the college, this time as assistant to the president.

I'd been back four years when I got a letter sporting
a Bangor postmark, with a string of lawyers' names in the
return address. The letter said that Jennifer Anne Pierce of
Wimsy, Maine, had died and that I was named in her will.
Please call.

It struck me funny at the time, that Jennifer Pierce
had named me in her will. My father had been Aunt
Jennifer's brother; I'd heard him speak of her half-a-dozen
times in his life, never kindly. I'd never met her, she having
moved to Maine about the time I was born. I understood
she was an artist and I gathered she was the black sheep of
the family— which made the joke even funnier. I wondered
if Jen Pierce the Elder had somehow known that her
namesake was the black sheep in *her* family.

I called Maine and spoke to my aunt's lawyer, fully
expecting to hear that my portion came to ten dollars cash
and a wheelbarrow-load of old paintings.

I heard *house*. I heard *ten acres*. I hung up the phone,
wrangled an out-of-season vacation from my boss and left
early next morning, driving nine hours straight, from
Baltimore to Wimsy.

The phone rang. I started, then snatched it up. "Jen
Pierce."

"Rand Funeral Home," the bored voice came down
the line. "I have an obit."

"Just a moment," I said, hurriedly saving Remember
Justin and opening a fresh file. "Go ahead."

It was a longish obituary, even though I took it

down in short-type, receiver trapped precariously between chin and left shoulder.

"Phone number?" I murmured and typed it at the end of the file. "Thank you."

"I'll have another one later on," the bored voice told me and hung up without goodbye. I went to the top of the file and started filling in the missing letters.

It was the house that brought me to Maine and it was the house that kept me in Maine. When my parents died the neat little suburban Baltimore bungalow with its tidy quarter-acre yard and conventional suburban furnishings went wholly to my sister Carol, the white sheep.

My share of the estate— two thousand, five hundred dollars and forty-five cents— arrived as a bank check in a lawyer's stiff buff envelope. The evening of its arrival, I went out and put twenty-five hundred dollars down on a midnight-black Camaro with red plush interior and treated myself to a cup of coffee with the forty-five cents.

The Camaro was my joy— I love driving fast, despite the various misfortunes automobiles have visited on me and mine. It now lived in the barn attached to the house— *my* house— double-undercoated against the predations of road salt and waxed 'til it gave back moonlight. It was an impractical car for Maine, especially for Maine winters. I knew that. But I kept it, the same way I kept the house, though I'd intended, at first, to sell.

I'd only intended to stay a couple days— just long enough to put the house on the market. But I woke up that first morning and there were birds singing outside the window of Jen Pierce's guest room. I put on my only pair of jeans, a polyester shirt and a denim jacket I found hanging by the kitchen door and went out to walk my land.

Later that day I called my boss and negotiated a six

month leave of absence, covered almost entirely by banked sick leave and unused vacation time.

Five months and fifteen days later, I called him again and tendered my resignation. Then I called my sister and asked her to turn the efficiency apartment that had been my home for the last six years back to the landlord and to ship my books, my stereo, my tapes, my files and my computer to Wimsy.

She didn't even ask me if I was okay.

"...Jen?"

I jumped, sending a line of mmmmmms along the middle of my obit, and stared up into Dan Skat's ratty face.

"What?"

"I *said*," he repeated, with a patented eye-roll. "Are we going to that meeting or aren't we?"

"Meeting's not 'til si— " I started, glancing involuntarily toward the newsroom clock: five fifty-five.

"Shit!" I grabbed my pad with one hand, my jacket and pocketbook with the other, pushed back from the computer and came to my feet.

"C'mon!" I snapped at Dan, running toward the door with my jacket slapping around my knees.

"Hey, I wasn't the one asleep at my terminal!" he yelled, running after.

"We'll take my car," he said, yanking open the stairwell door and stepping back for me to pass. "It's closer."

# 3

IT WAS STANDING ROOM only at the Wimsy Elementary School auditorium.

Dan and I split up at the door: he to creep through the crowd, grabbing shots as he saw them; I to wedge into a back corner, pad and pen at the ready, my pocketbook a dead weight dragging down my left shoulder.

I measure in at precisely six foot: tall for a woman, even in Baltimore, where they grow 'em a tad high. In Maine, I'm a gangling, gawky giant, towering a full head over most grown men. The position at the far back of the room suited me perfectly— a clear sighting across the sea of bobbing heads, down to the stage up front, where Wimsy's three selectpeople sat behind a scarred table, looking bored, serious and sleepy, respectively.

The clock above the stage read six-oh-five.

I looked over the crowd, found Harry Pelletier and Maurice DuChamp side by side in the third row. Reverend Stern sat front and center, the prime first-row chairs on either side of him vacant. If Scott and Merry were present, I didn't spot them, though Merry's white-blonde mop should have cut through that mob of peaked caps and shades of brown like Twin Rivers Light through a fog-bank.

The acoustics were about what you'd expect and nobody was really taking care to talk low. First Selectwoman Marjorie Lavoie had to pound her gavel several times— hard— against its battered block of wood to get the rumpus down to where she could be heard yelling for "Quiet!"

Quiet, of a sort, descended. The sea of heads grew still, caps pointed toward the front. There was some rustling and throat-clearing; Marjorie laid down the gavel and crossed her arms on the table.

"This meeting is called to resolve a dispute over repair of an existing barn at Johnson's Farm off the Point Road. We have a petition." She held it at arm's-length above her head— a sheaf of dog-eared papers maybe six sheets thick— and whacked it back to the table top.

"Who's here to speak for the petitioners?" she asked, just like she didn't know.

Front and center, Butchie Stern raised his hand.

"Reverend." Marjorie nodded. "This meeting will hear objections to Scott Ash's formal and legal request to the town that he be allowed to repair a barn on his property."

Reverend Stern stood— no, he *rose*— oil-smooth and elegant in a dark suit. He made a slight, European-looking bow toward the three selectfolks, then pivoted to face the meeting.

His shirt was white, his tie a swirl of silky blues. A gold tie bar held it firmly in place. He wore a gold band on the third finger of his left hand. It glinted when he raised his hands to the crowd.

My fingers twitched on the slick plastic barrel of my ballpoint.

*"Friends,"* I muttered at the back of my throat.

"Friends," Butchie Stern intoned from the front of the auditorium. He lowered his hands on a slow beat of three and looked out gravely across the crowd.

"Friends," he said again. "We're hardworking folks in this town. We admire industry, we admire care for the land— and we admire privacy. There are those of you sitting out there right now saying to yourselves, 'Young fella wants to patch his barn— good for him. No business of mine.'"

Butchie smiled, sad and soft.

"Nor should it be any business of yours, what a man does with his own property. But we're also a moral town— a church-going town— " He raised his right hand and pointed dramatically toward the west corner of the room. "There are three houses of God sitting cheek by jowl on Church Street. Come Sunday morning those three churches are going to be full, just like every Sunday morning." He brought his hand down and leaned toward the crowd, lowering his voice, but not so much I still couldn't hear every word, back in my corner.

"Scott Ash's barn is the business of every church-going, moral member of this community." He straightened, face showing sadness and determination.

"Scott Ash is, by his own admission, a Wiccan. His— wife— calls herself a High Priestess. In plain, everyday language, Scott and Merry Ash are witches." Butchie held up a quick hand, gold band glinting.

"It's no business of yours, what beliefs a man chooses to hold. After all, those are three very different churches downtown, and the Baptists don't always agree with the Catholics, or the Catholics with the Congregationalists. But we all read from the same Book, friends. And we all look to the same— the only— God."

It was fortunate for Reverend Stern, I thought sourly, as he paused for effect, that there was no Unitarian church in town, much less a synagogue. One Book and one God. Yep. I scrawled, the sound of pen scratching paper loud in the rapt stillness.

"There may be those of you," Butchie said gently, "who either do not believe in witches, or are ignorant of the rites of witches. Let me tell you something about the— religion— of Wicca, the religion in which Scott Ash's— wife—

claims to be a High Priestess.

"Witches practice an orgiastic religion. During their sabbats— their celebrations— men and women dance naked together. They have sex with multiple partners as part of their—worship. They repudiate the true Word of the true God and offer up their lewd behavior in sacrifice to a goddess— to a *female* god." Butchie paused. "And also to a male god," he added, too quietly. "Who is often shown wearing— horns." He sighed.

"There is more— all well documented. But I will not offend the sensibilities of the moral people of this town by reciting the darker rites performed at these meetings. Suffice to say that privacy— the deep privacy found inside a barn on an isolated farm— is necessary for these practices. And it is the business of every person in this room— the business of every person in this town!— to ask Scott Ash what it is he intends to do with his barn."

Reverend Stern folded his hands, turned, half-bowed to the selectpeople and sat. The auditorium might have been filled with wax dollies, each pinned fatally through the heart.

There was a slight rustle from the eighth row, the last seat by the far aisle. A man came slowly to his feet: beat-up jeans jacket open over a plaid flannel shirt; clean shaven; pale brown hair combed neatly behind his ears.

"I'm Scott Ash," he said, and there was a drawling edge of bluegrass to his voice. He looked around the room, taking his time about it: southern slow and a shade puzzled-looking. A camera flashed as he turned his face toward Dan Skat's position, and he reached up to rub his neck before looking back toward the table on the stage.

"Well, now, that's a good question," he said, "what we're going to be doing with the barn. I guess I should've explained when I filled out the form." He looked around again, moved broad denim-covered shoulders in an apologetic shrug.

"See," he said earnestly, slipping his hands into his jeans pockets, "we were planning on keeping the sheep in it."

From somewhere near my corner came a half-choke of laughter. In the third row, Harry flung her hand into the air.

"Meeting sees Haroldene Pelletier," Marjorie Lavoie said, with commendable steadiness.

"I move Scott Ash be allowed to mend his barn and get his animals under roof!" Harry shouted. Reverend Stern actually turned in his chair to glare at her.

"Second!" Maurice yelled, bouncing to his feet before Marjorie had time to open her mouth.

The crowd went wild.

\*\*\*

KAREN'S COMPUTER laboriously loaded its spell-checker as I leaned back in the cranky, too-short chair, rubbed my eyes and felt the vibration from the press in the basement rumble through my bones.

Marjorie had quickly snatched control of the meeting back from my two elderly reprobates, called for discussion and then a vote, all proper and parliamentary.

The hour-long discussion ranged from Johnson Farm history, to the chances of the weather holding, to the number of sheep in Scott's herd and the fact that the winter hay was already rolled and stowed, neat and workmanlike, under blue tarp in the near pasture.

Nobody mentioned witchcraft, or dancing naked. Nobody mentioned sex, except as it pertained to sheep.

Nobody mentioned abortion.

And when Marjorie Lavoie finally called for a show of hands, the meeting voted one-hundred-fifty-three to six in favor of Scott Ash being allowed to repair his barn.

Karen's Computer beeped peevishly for my attention. I pried my eyes open and okay'd the spelling of "Congregationalist." The computer hiccupped and continued its search.

I sighed. As much as I was ever proud of the work I did for the *Voice,* I was was proud of this piece. It was chockfull of good quotes, glimmers of Wimsy personalities— and it didn't hurt that Butchie Stern had hung himself on his own length of rope, without a shred of help from anyone else.

"Am I going to have that story before deadline, Miz Pierce?" Bill Jacques, being courtly.

I ground my teeth and summoned up my sweetest secretarial voice.

"Just spell-checking, Mr. Jacques. We wouldn't want to hand in a shoddy piece of work."

"Hey, third desk is schizophrenic!" Milt yelled from first, fingers never faltering in their frenzied dash across his keyboard.

"That explains why she does twice as much work as you," Bill said in a tone of broad enlightenment.

Carly the copy editor gave one of her hard shouts of laughter— "HA!"— without lifting her eyes from the screen. Milt, prudently, retreated to silence.

Karen's Computer announced that spell-checking was complete. I saved the document, copied it, reformatted the copy, saved it and hit control-alt-S, the sequence that would theoretically send the story from my computer to Bill Jacques'.

"Transmitting now," I sang out. "Barn-point-Jen."

There was a longish pause, broken by the clatter of Milt's keys and the rumble of the press.

"Got it!" Bill called.

I nodded and began to shut down for the night, tidying my desk, checking the calendar, pushing papers into file folders, file folders into the crammed desk holder— old habits, secretarial habits... comforting habits.

Last, I shut down Karen's Computer, breathing a prayer for its safe resurrection, come Sunday; got up and shrugged into my jacket. On the way out, I paused at Bill Jacques' desk.

"Any questions on that?" I asked, fingering car keys out of my pocketbook.

"Hmm?" He looked at me over the rim of his half-glasses, not quite focusing. "Nope, it's clean. 'night."

"Goodnight," I said, loud enough to include the whole newsroom. I walked out into the hall, holding back the sigh by main force. "It's clean" was high praise from Bill Jacques. I tried to remember that as I worked the night latch on the front door and crossed the parking lot to the Camaro.

# 4

THE HOUSE AT WIMSY Point is vintage New England farmhouse, with the barn attached to the main house by an unheated hallway— the "ell," according to Harry Pelletier.

In the old days, when winters were rugged and livestock lived at home, the ell made it possible for the farmer to get from house to barn without the risk of getting lost in the weather: a practical necessity and one more coup for Yankee Ingenuity.

I parked the Camaro in the barn and walked down the dark ell. At the end of the hall, I pushed open the plank door and stepped into the muted light of the kitchen. The door swung back on its spring, whacking against the frame.

I hung my pocketbook and jacket on pegs by the ell door, crossed the kitchen and opened the round-shouldered refrigerator. A block of sharp cheddar whispered my name; I emerged from the fridge with it in my left hand and a bottle of cheap white wine in my right.

Briefly, I cubed cheese and poured wine, flung a handful of crackers onto the plate as an afterthought and carried my snack upstairs.

My room is on the second floor, at the back; the only room in the house that's different now than it was when Aunt Jen died.

It had been a storeroom, of sorts, a big drafty place that was home to a collection of half-finished paintings, oldish books and older trunks. I moved that stuff up to the main attic, where it vanished among more of the same, and turned my attention and five hundred dollars from my retirement fund toward making the storeroom home.

The room had been insulated: pink fiberglass with brown paper backing stapled into the wall channels; the floor was bare plank. I hung sheetrock, painted, laid padding and carpet, built bookshelves and installed a ceiling fan. I splurged for a second phone line, bought curtains and shades for the old-fashioned double-hung windows, dared to move an old pine rocker up from a dark corner of the parlor, pillaged a bright wool afghan from the back of the sofa and a brass-based reading lamp from beside the china cabinet.

When my stuff arrived from Baltimore, the computer and printer went into the desk I'd ordered special from a store in New York. The stereo slid into the place I'd built for it, cassette tapes lining the shelf above. The rest of the shelves were filled with books.

I'd painted the door yellow on the hall-side— wildly out of place in an ordinary New England farmhouse— and always kept it shut. Nobody went through that door but me— not even the cat. I juggled wine and cheese-plate; worked the latch.

And was home.

\*\*\*

I SET THE GLASS ON the pottery tile, put the plate on the far side of the mouse pad. A flick of two switches and my computer sang to life. I sank into my chair and closed my eyes.

A couple lifetimes ago, back in Baltimore, I'd been moderator of a call-in talk line. A precursor of the 900-numbers advertised in the back of men's magazines, callers chatted about current events, the weather, books, music, clubs, history, religion, and any other more-or-less non-sexual topic.

Needless to say, Chat Hostess wasn't one of my longer-lasting jobs, but it was one of my favorites. From four-to-eight daily, I sat in a cramped attic room, ensconced in the most luxurious chair I'd ever experienced, 'phones hugging my ears, mike kissing my lips, eyes front and center, watching a blank computer screen. When a call clicked in, a dot would appear on the screen.

Inez, the black girl who did eight-to-midnight, bitched that she never could match those silly dots with a human voice. She ran her shift eyes closed and called everybody "Honey."

I ran things different; placed every name and the location of every caller. Because the screen wasn't a random array of unrelated dots to me. To me, the screen was a window on a classy bar-and-lounge. I had the table pattern in my head, the location of the potted palms, the way the bar was mahogany and glowed under the soft lighting, the orderly march of stools against the brass foot rail. A caller didn't jump in from nowhere, a random, nameless dot, he strolled through the front door, took a seat, settled in and waved for a drink.

The scene was so real to me I'd often tell people where they were sitting— it got to be a game among the regulars. It drove Inez crazy to get one of my callers on her shift.

"Where am I sitting?" the caller would ask, or, worse, try to order a drink. Inez would clench her eyes real tight and swap the Goucher-girl accent for pure Lexington Street.

"Honey, Jenny run that dive an' it shut down when she go home. My momma din't raise me to work in no bar."

The night they pulled the lines, I stayed after time in The Chair, phones and mike in place, eyes leaking tears, staring at the screen.

"What are you doing, if I may ask?" Inez put her hand on my shoulder and frowned into my face.

"Closing the place down," I whispered, mentally pulling blinds, wiping the bar, shutting off the jukebox, turning down the lights.

"Oh." Inez sat on the arm of The Chair, eyes for once wide open on the screen, waiting while I tidied up. When there was nothing else to do, I left the keys on the bar and, finally— forever— walked out the door.

Then I pulled off the headphones and mike, coiled the wire and put the unit on the keyboard.

"All done?" Inez asked. I nodded.

"Okay." She stood, reaching down to take my cold hand in her warm brown fingers. "Let's go over to the Owl and get something to eat. Glass of wine."

I pried myself out of the chair and tried to smile down into her face. "I thought your momma didn't let you go to no bars."

"She don't let me *work* in no bars," she corrected sternly. "My momma ain't nobody's fool."

My computer beeped ready. Eyes still closed, I reached out and tapped in "talk."

There was a whisper of pause, then a click as the modem came live and dialed. Some miles south, in the October city of Boston, Massachusetts, a phone rang, eerie soft within the computer. Then the connect blared, followed by a gong. I opened my eyes and entered my password.

The Net opened and I kited in. First stop was the post office: there were four electronic letters in my virtual mailbox and the latest issue of Cyberspace Review, a "hyper-mag" with an editorial stance somewhere between *Time* and *Mad*. I downloaded everything with a stab and a mouse-click, then took a second to look about me.

The same over-vivid imagination that built Jen's Place gave me a Net honeycombed with hallways, rich with stores, lecture halls, and neighborhood beer-and-grills— not a particularly unique take. Many Net users thought of the BBS as a shopping mall, still others as a compact and orderly small city. I'd met some who simply saw a screen bordered in icons; flat white words displayed against a silent blue ground.

But not many.

I reached for my wine, sipped and decided. I hadn't been to the Chat Shack in more than a week. Might as well stop in the live-line area and gather some gossip.

In my mind, I turned up the collar of the leather jacket I owned only in fantasy, pushed my hands deep into the fleece-lined pockets and walked down a particular, bright-lit hallway.

In my room, back in midnight Maine, my right hand moved the mouse: up, grab, drag, click.

Chat Shack bloomed around me.

\*\*\*

RAFFER902 AND ANGELGABE were arguing. The other occupants of the room— Scarlett, MagikMan and Fleeny— seemed to be trying to have an actual discussion, but well-spelled, punctuated, reasoned discourse was no match for the all-caps screaming going on in the back corner.

NO WAY YOU DINK BOND IS THE ULTIMATE THE BEST EVERYBODY ELSE IS JUST

IMITATION YOUR JUST PISSED YOU DIDNT THINK
OF HIM FIRST.

GEORGE SMILEY'S THE MAN, MAN! HE'S THE
ONE CALLS THE SHOTS, MAKES THE PLANS.
BOND'S A DORK, MAN. SHAKEN NOT STIRRED.
WHAT A WIMP.

BOND IS NOT A WIMP! Raffer shrieked, goaded
into punctuation.

I wandered over to the others.

"Magik. Fleeny."

Scarlett's poison-sweet murmur hit the screen first:
"Well, look who's here— Frontier Woman."

"Good evening, Jennifer," said Fleeny.

"Jenmeister!" MagikMan shouted. "Long time, no
type!"

I grinned while my fingers danced. "Busy, busy."

"In MAINE?" demanded Magik. "I figured you'd be
snowed in for the winter and settling down for a couple days
of hot computing."

MagikMan is a self-proclaimed "PR-guy" from down
Daytona Beach way. Sun all the time, so he tells it, and a tan
down to *here*. He writes murder mysteries "on the side."
Claims it helps him keep perspective.

A REAL SPY HAS BRAINS, NOT JUST
REACTIONS, Angel told Raffer at volume, overriding
Fleeny's well-bred inquiry into my health.

WHAT DO YOU KNOW ABOUT IT ANYWAY,
yelled Raffer. NOTHING YOUVE WRITTEN HAS EVER
SOLD OR EVER WILL!

"Oh, oh," said Magik.

"That's torn it," Scarlett agreed. Fleeny didn't say
anything. She didn't have to.

"Let's blow this place," I said quickly. "Meet you at the

Horned Moon."

The Moon's over on Religion Street; this hour on a Thursday night it would be under the watchful eye of SpringRayn, who tolerated no capital-letter conversations in her bar.

"Good idea," said Magik, and was gone.

"The Moon," Fleeny murmured, possibly to remind herself, because she didn't wait for verification before blinking out of the Shack.

Scarlett was likewise gone, leaving a cooed, "Coming, Jenny?" behind her.

I shot one more look at the combatants in the corner, moved the mouse— and flew.

# 5

THE PHONE SHRIEKED.

I groaned and pulled the covers over my head, nestling shamelessly into my own warmth.

The phone rang again.

"'s Friday," I muttered to my knees. "I can sleep all day." That had been the logic by which I had purchased the right to prowl The Net 'til four, exploring back hallways and poking my nose into late-night cafes.

The phone rang again. Obviously, there was only one way to make it stop.

I stuck an arm out into the cold air, groped toward the nightstand, snatched the receiver and hauled it back under the covers just as the fourth ring began.

"What?" I demanded crankily.

"You still asleep?" Harry Pelletier yelled in my ear.

"It'd be nice. In fact, I think I'll try to go back to sleep, now that God-awful noise has stopped."

"It's nine o'clock," Harry said in a voice that added, *and I've been up for hours.*

"No work. Sleep the whole damn' day if I want to." I yawned. "*And* I want to."

"No, you don't," Harry told me. "You get on up and fix yourself a cup of coffee. I'll be by in half-an-hour to get you."

"Get me," I repeated, puzzlement nibbling at the edges of exhaustion. "What for?"

"So you can be at the barn-raisin'."

"Barn-raising?" I opened my eyes inside the warm tent of bedclothes and frowned. "What barn-raising? I don't— no.

Oh, no. Harry, I am not going to the Ash's barn-raising.
This is my day off and I intend to spend it productively,
which in this case means sleeping until noon."

"Whole town's going to be there, what I heard. Look
like you was on Butchie Sterns' side, you didn't come lend a
hand."

I closed my eyes.

"Harry."

"Yep."

"You're a low, evil-minded woman and I don't know
how my aunt put up with you."

"Well, see, Jen didn't need no raisin' by the time she
come up here. Knew what was due the neighbors and never
grudged it."

My eyes popped open in sheer surprise and sleep
vanished entirely. "Spoiled, am I?"

"Unheedful— but I think you can learn. I'm by in
half-an-hour, you hear me?"

"I hear you," I said, but I might as well saved my
breath.

Harry'd already hung up.

\*\*\*

THE LONG DRIVEWAY off the Point Road was
lined with pickup trucks. Harry pulled in behind a shiny
red Chevy with two rifles in the gun rack, killed the engine
and gave me a look.

"Looks like the county fair."

Harry nodded. "Plenty of hands. Some of them
won't be no use, understand." She jerked her head at the red
truck. "Tommy Boucher ain't good for nothing but
drinking beer and giving bad advice. But we should have

'em under roof by nightfall, regardless."

Stifling a sigh, I worked the tricky latch and slid out of the truck. The *Voice's* spare camera swung from my shoulder; notebook and pen crammed into the right-hand pocket of my jacket. As long as I was forced into a barn-raising, I'd reflected sourly, I might as well get paid for it.

I slammed the door and walked around to the driver's side, watching as Harry climbed out, favoring her left knee. She looked up just as she closed the door and gave me a tight grin.

"Coming on to rain, I guess," she said, shrugging off the flawlessly blue October sky with godlike unconcern.

"Can you walk all the way down to the house?" I demanded, which I knew was against the rules, but dammit, she was sixty if she was a day— and none of those years had been easy.

Harry opened her eyes wide. "Been walking all my life," she said just as a brown pickup bearing the legend, "Old Smoky Orchard, Heirloom Maine Apples," pulled up and parked.

"Here's Morris," Harry said then. "Wait a tick and we'll all walk down together."

Both brown doors popped open. Morris emerged from the driver's side with a grin and a wave.

From the passenger's side came the most gorgeous man I'd seen in my life.

He was definitely not Wimsy; I had five bucks that said he wasn't even Maine. What he was, was tall— six-two, maybe— working-guy lean, with a careless, gleaming, golden mane, blue eyes to drown in, chiseled chin and the cheekbones of a rock legend. He shut the door gently and came around the truck, displaying a set of perfectly even, perfectly white teeth.

"Jennifer, Harry, this is Craig, my new hand."

"Pleasure," Harry said, touching the brim of her hat.

"Hi," I said shortly. Beautiful men set my teeth on edge, and send me reeling through a time-warp to high school, where, tall and skinny and plainer than that wall, I was on the receiving end of ceaseless ridicule from handsome teenage boys and their doll-perfect girlfriends.

"Harry Pelletier," Morris was telling Craig, "our neighbor across the north planting."

"Ma'am," Craig said, holding out his hand with that too-perfect smile. Harry gave him a brief shake and another nod.

"Jenny Pierce writes for the newspaper," Morris said, with avuncular pride. "She's a real barnburner, all right. You two might have something to talk about, both being from the south like you are."

Craig's smile widened. He extended a tan, ringless hand. There was nothing to do but give the man a shake and a "Welcome to Wimsy." His palm was tough with callus.

"Thank you," he said, keeping my hand for a second longer than I wanted and smiling down into my eyes.

"Well," Morris was saying merrily to Harry, "I guess this'll set Butchie up proper."

"Think we ought to ask him to send up a prayer for the roof," Harry said, sliding her arm matter-of-factly through his and moving down the drive. "Only be neighborly."

Morris cackled and Craig fell in beside me, two steps to the rear of the older couple.

"So," he said, inclining his head toward mine, "what part of the south are you from?"

"Baltimore," I said and got the expected frown and a shake of that sun-blessed head.

"Midcoast— the largest city in the state of Maryland," I explained, with the patience of frequent retellings. "On the Chesapeake Bay. Below the Mason-Dixon Line. Next to Washington, D.C."

D.C., he'd heard of; the frown relaxed back into a smile. "Hey, that's really south!" The smile went into a grin of pure deviltry. "For up this way, anyhow."

I grinned back, feeling the first stir of actual liking. "Your turn," I said. "How far south?"

"You probably never heard of it," he said, feigning apology while the blue eyes danced.

"Try me."

"Well— Rhode Island."

I choked. "Rhode Island!"

"Providence," he added, making a clean breast.

I took a hard breath against a quiver of laughter and gave him my sternest secretarial glare. "That's east."

"Southeast, now. Southeast." He made a soothing gesture with his big tanned hand. "This is Maine, remember. The ocean is east. Canada's north. Everything else is south."

"Including California," I agreed.

Craig blinked at me, drawing together brows three shades darker than his hair. "California," he said thoughtfully, "ain't that foreign?"

I did laugh then and shook my head. "Close enough. What're you doing 'way up here?"

"Well, right now I'm picking apples and bossing the crew. Uncle Maury wants me to stay on after picking and help out with the winter spruce-up. Then next year I'll be helping with the pruning and all."

It was my turn to blink and flash a quick look at the back of Maurice's head as he chattered to Harry in front of us.

"Uncle Maury?"

"I'm a pretty distant relation," he said, eyes moving off mine to scan ahead. "Something like eighteenth cousin twice removed— his father and my great-aunt went to Sunday School together." He laughed, too hearty, and looked back at me.

"What brings you to Maine, a real southerner like yourself?"

"Actually," I said slowly, "a relative. My aunt died and left me her house."

"Not too bad," he returned and asked the hottest question of the last few years with just the right touch of bitterness. "She leave you a job, too?"

"Lucked into a job at the paper."

"That's right, Uncle Maury said that. Reporter, huh? That must be exciting."

"In Wimsy," I said, as we came round a pool of pickups and into the dooryard, "this is as exciting as it gets."

Scott Ash was standing in a knot of men, talking and shaping air with his hands. There was a glint of silver on his left hand. He turned to point at something up the drive and caught sight of us.

Harry waved. Scott stared, the high color draining out of his cheeks, leaving them a kind of sickly beige.

He was staring right at me.

I stopped like I'd walked into a stone wall. Scott had no reason to love me, but he had no reason to be terrified of me, either.

"I'm going around back and make myself useful," Craig said, but I barely registered the words. I was staring at Scott, and Scott was staring at me.

Then, suddenly, he wasn't. He'd turned back to his group of cronies and was shaking his head at a paunchy young man in a stretched-out red T-shirt, patiently reworking the air with long, capable fingers.

    I gulped air, abruptly realizing that I was shaking. Straightening the camera strap on my shoulder, I turned blindly toward the left and the sound of hammering.

# 6

"...GOOD STORY!" THE VOICE originated somewhere near the edge of my left shoulder. It was a bright voice, perky and clear, loud over the banging of the hammers.

I half-choked on a gasp and turned my head: left and down. "I'm sorry?" I stammered.

Molasses-brown eyes looked up at me through a fly-away tangle of platinum curls.

"I said," she said, "'that was a good story!' You're Jennifer Pierce, right?"

I nodded.

"Merry Ash." She stuck a hand up and out. I hunched my shoulder to keep the camera strap in place, stuck my own hand out and shook.

"Hi." I said, graciousness frozen by the memory of Scott's face, color draining away, eyes fear-wide....

"Are you okay?" Merry Ash asked, small fingers hard around mine.

I blinked, made a serious effort and yanked myself firmly into the present.

"I'm fine," I said, dredging up a grin. "Just the shock of somebody actually praising the *Voice*."

She grinned back and let my hand go.

"I wasn't praising the *Voice*, "she said. "I was praising your work. It's hard to go to a meeting like that and come away with a coherent story, much less a story that tells exactly what happened."

She talked like she knew the game, which was

interesting. But there was something else interesting, too.

"I didn't see you at the meeting."

The grin this time was crooked. "Scott wouldn't let me go. Said I'd only get torqued, listening to Reverend Slime's witch-bashing. He was right, too. I don't think I could have kept it during his little chat on Wiccan rites." She screwed up her face in what I took to be an imitation of Reverend Stern's more sanctimonious face.

"An *orgiastic* religion," she intoned nasally, "worshipping a *female* god!" She let the pose drop and shook her head. "The man needs professional help. Scott said you could just *tell* the idea of a goddess made his skin crawl."

"He didn't seem too taken with the notion," I allowed, Maine-dry. Merry laughed, then sobered.

"Do you believe he had the nerve to come here today?" she demanded. "All dressed up in a gray silk suit, which is exactly *my* idea of what to wear while hammering nails."

This I did not believe. "Butchie Stern is helping patch your barn?"

"Did I say that? No, he's just wandering around with a long face, staring at the folks who came to work, shaking his head and sighing soulfully." Merry ran both hands through her whirlwind curls; the wide silver band on her left hand matched Scott's.

"Could be worse, I guess," she said. "He could've brought his crew down and had them march all over the front yard with their dead-baby posters."

"There's that." I hitched the camera strap on my shoulder, sighing at the familiar, muscle-deep cramp. "Listen," I said to Merry, "do you mind if I take a couple pictures, maybe talk to some people?"

"On the clock?" She flung a hand out. "Help yourself.

I'll be around, if there's anything you need." She grinned. "Why not interview Reverend Slime? Ask him how he finds the day's festivities." The grin widened. "Might go find him myself and invite him to stay after for some of that old-time religion."

I tried to picture Butchie Stern standing as one of thirteen in Circle. Imagination failed. I shook my head.

"Be pouring gas on a fire."

"Scott would say so, too," Merry agreed and tipped her head. "Where are you from originally?"

"Baltimore," I said and waited for the blank stare.

The molasses-brown eyes lit. "Hey, no kidding? There was a *great* bookstore on Charles Street, about a block from Walters Art Gallery— you know the one?"

"Rubrik Books," I said and she snapped her fingers.

"That's it! I spent *days* in that place." She put her hand quickly on my sleeve. "Come over sometime and we'll talk Baltimore," she said. "Right now, I've got to run and you're on the clock. Later."

"Later," I said, and watched her move off toward the house. She had quite a stride on her, for a short girl.

Behind me, a guy yelled something and another guy yelled back. A chain saw cranked, died and caught. And above it all the hammers hammered, an impenetrable roof of sound.

\*\*\*

I WANDERED AROUND LIKE a kid at the fair, gawking at the exhibits and occasionally taking pictures. The *Voice's* extra camera is a lightweight autofocus Dan Skat dismisses as an "instant camera," which means it's just about my speed. I got a great shot of Tommy Boucher with his finger in Butchie Stern's face and another of Merry Ash, swinging her hammer with a grin. I grabbed a shot of an end pole rising from the hands of a dozen bearded men in caps, and another of Scott Ash, standing a little apart from the general ruckus, hands on hips, watching it all through narrowed eyes.

Supper was shouted about the time I ran out of film. I leaned against the side of a pickup truck and cracked the camera, pried out the used roll, dropped it in its canister, then held it in one hand while I rummaged in the camera bag for the spare roll, spilling old filters and pencil stubs onto the ground.

I reloaded finally, gathered up the junk and dumped it back in the bag before wandering into the yard, notebook in hand.

I found Deputy Sheriff Bruce Gagnon braced against a saw horse, ham sandwich in one hand and beer in the other, looking— incomplete— out of uniform.

"Sheriff. Expecting trouble today?"

Bruce grunted. "Not unless some damnfool drinks too much and falls off the roof-beam." He eyed the notebook. "This is my day off. I'm here as a private citizen, helping out a neighbor."

"Sure," I said, giving him my blandest smile. I waved the notebook at the rest of the suppertime crowd. "Kind of amazing, don't you think? All these people turning up to help."

He bit off half his sandwich and swigged some beer to help it on its way.

"Don't think it's amazing at all," he said. "Wimsy folks are always willing to help a neighbor."

"You don't think this has anything to do with Reverend Stern calling the special meeting, then? Community reaction, that sort of thing?"

Bruce gave me a hard stare. "I don't think this has anything at all to do with the Reverend," he said and finished his sandwich.

That was pretty much the party line. Folks who were willing to talk at all talked about neighbor helping neighbor and community support that was a Maine tradition, born in the frigid womb of a hundred northern winters, when each town was isolated, cast upon its own resources. Wholesome, uplifting stuff— Monday morning good news for the top of page two.

I snapped Harry Pelletier deep in conversation with Merry Ash, then went looking for Scott.

Supper was breaking up; people were going back to their work stations by ones, twos and sixes.

I scanned the yard, but didn't see my man, so I headed for the barn, notebook and pen in my right hand, camera bag banging my hip. My left shoulder was bitching; I ground my teeth and forcibly ignored it.

"Jenny! Hey, Jenny!" The voice was marginally familiar: male— and gaining on me.

I stopped and turned around.

"Hey, hi," Craig said, smiling his perfect smile. His mane was wind-whipped and he'd peeled to a faded blue T-shirt. If possible, he looked more gorgeous than he had this morning.

"Hi," I said, not very enthusiastically.

"So, how's it going?" he asked. "The reporting?"

"It's going okay. How's the barn-building?"

"Good— it's going good. Listen, I didn't want to let you get away without asking— you, umm— You busy tomorrow?"

It took a moment to sink in, and when it did I had to choke down a shout of laughter.

"I thought maybe we could go over to Waterville," Craig said into my quavering silence. "You could, you know, show me the sights." He grinned. "Be the neighborly thing to do."

*This is not happening,* I told myself, and then: *I am going to strangle Morris DuChamp. Oh yes I am.*

"I'm really sorry," I said, trying to sound like it. "Tomorrow's bad, and— " better cut off the inevitable, "I work Sunday."

"Oh." He didn't seem especially heartbroken. "Well, maybe some other time."

"Maybe," I didn't-agree pleasantly. I shifted my feet and half-leaned away.

"Going back?" Craig asked, moving his hand toward the yard and all the commotion.

"Going to try a shot around the other side," I smiled at him and moved off, stretching my legs and pretending not to hear his "Hey— "

I went around the far end of the barn, heading for the tidy rolls of tarp-covered hay, walking away from Craig more than I was looking for Scott, who should, after all, be in the thick of things, or maybe in the house, taking a well-earned breather.

I hit the edge of the barn, and heard the sound of someone running hard over dry grass, breath rasping noisily.

Big city instinct took over. I slammed back against the barn siding, poised to run and pretending to be invisible.

Scott Ash tore around the corner, running flat out toward the house. His face was white under the farmer tan. He never turned his head.

Prudence dictated that I run as fast as my legs would carry me in Scott's wake.

I ran along his back trail, sprinted across the tiny

clearing, following the broken grass around the last hay-roll.

A man was lying on the ground just behind the roll. Gray suit, white shirt, blue tie.

I moved, digging in the camera bag for the red filter. Dropping to my knees, I held it over his mouth with one hand while I groped for his wrist with the other.

No pulse.

No breath fogging the lens.

Butchie Stern was stone dead, near as I could tell. His eyes were open, staring straight up; his face perfectly bland.

The blue tie was crumpled untidily beneath his chin. I reached out automatically to straighten it.

"Don't touch him!" Bruce Gagnon snarled from behind me. "Move away now and let me see what we've got."

# 7

"MEDICAL EXAMINER COMING?" EMT Deb Joliceur asked Bruce. I edged a little closer to their huddle, straining my ears.

Bruce shook his head. "Called it in. Told 'em he had a bad heart and was seeing Dr. Chilson regular. M.E. said to arrange transport."

Deb nodded. "Okay," she said and waved to her partner, a blocky man with a dark mustache who looked familiar, though I couldn't put my mind on his name.

Deftly, they lifted Butchie onto a stretcher, draped him with a patched white sheet and loaded it. The man went into the back of the truck with the stretcher and Deb swung the door closed, hauling down hard on the latch. She walked to the front of the truck.

Shortly after, Wimsy Rescue moved out and we— the ones left alive— stood in a ragged circle and stared at each other.

"Now what?" Tommy Boucher wondered loudly.

"I say we get back to work," said a unfamiliar voice from the left.

"Back to work?" That was Chris Poulin, Wimsy's handyman-at-large. "But a guy *died*."

"Well, it wasn't like he was helpin' any," Tommy said. "Jakey's right. No reason we can't finish the job today."

"Weather can't hold forever," Millard Freeman observed in his dry, old-Maine way. He pushed the cap back off his forehead and glanced up at the sky. "Full moon tonight. If you boys are willin' to step out, we'll finish her up, right enough."

"All right... Yeah... Let's do it...." The day was won, easy as that; the men moved off, talk already turning toward the mechanics of construction.

Glancing around, I saw Harry Pelletier standing over by the first hayroll, looking down at the mashed grass, hands shoved deep into the pockets of her jeans. I walked over and faced her across the place where Butchie Stern had lain.

"Should somebody tell his wife?" I asked, wondering as I did if Bruce Gagnon would perform that office, or if maybe she had friends among the people gathered here....

"Wife?" Harry looked up sharply, eyes narrowed.

"Wife," I repeated, hearing the surprise in my own voice. "Or widow. Whatever." My aunt's best friend continued to stare at me, narrow-eyed.

"For God's sake, Harry, the man wore a wedding band!"

There was a short pause before she ducked her head and moved her shoulders. "Yep. He did do that." She sighed, pulled off her cap with one hand and ran the other through her flattened hair.

"He did do that," she repeated, and settled the cap again before looking back at me.

"I'll tell her," she said, and started walking.

I grabbed her shoulder as she went past. "You don't have to do it," I said. "I was just wondering if maybe she had friends here, somebody who— "

"I'll tell her," Harry said, limping steadily onward. I went with her, matching my stride to hers. "Know her as well as anyone else." She glanced sideways into my face. "Went to elementary school together."

The phrase grabbed me by the ear. I stopped at the edge of the barn and stared at her.

"You, and Butchie and Butchie's— wife."

Harry nodded. "All the same age, within a month or two." Her mouth tightened. "Getting old's a bitch," she said. "You grab a ride home with Morris, now. Hear me?"

"I hear you, Harry."

She nodded and turned away, stumping toward a bunch of guys gathered 'round a saw horse. They stepped back and let her by.

I watched 'til she disappeared around the first truck in the dooryard.

Then I went looking for Scott.

\*\*\*

THEY WERE IN THE kitchen of the old farmhouse, in full view of the window. Scott was kneeling on the battered linoleum floor, his face in Merry's lap. She was sitting at attention, backbone inches from the chair-rest, eyes closed. From where I stood on the porch, I could see his shoulders shaking; see her hand move in long, slow strokes along his hair, over and over.

I turned away from the window and stepped lightly across the porch. In the dooryard, I moved the camera bag from my left shoulder to my right, touched the notebook in my pocket and nodded. It's just over two miles from the old Johnson place to Wimsy Point— what my father used to call "a nice stretch of the legs."

I started walking.

\*\*\*

BY THE TIME I HIT the top of my drive, I had the story framed and roughed in. It was Page One stuff now, by the *Voice's* standards: Butchie Stern might have been a gadfly, but he had inarguably been a prominent resident of the town.

I paused at the battered aluminum mailbox on its listing post. "Jennifer Pierce" read the flaking pink letters, "RR3 Box 2612."

Jennifer Pierce.

I stood with my hand on the rusty dome, remembering the first time I had seen this mailbox, my name carefully hand-lettered in what had once doubtlessly been a pure painter's crimson. Harry Pelletier had been with me.

"Well," she'd observed, with a certain gallows dryness. "Save you some work, changin' the name."

I'd shaken myself then, as I did now, and yanked open the warped hatch to look for my mail. In Baltimore, single women living alone did the possible to hide those facts. The tags on every mailbox I'd ever had, the plate on my apartment door, my listing in the telephone book— all, all, every one, read J. Pierce. J for John, you understand. Jason. Or Joshua.

And here was Jennifer Pierce, proudly proclaiming herself to the world. It boggled the big-city mindset. Sometimes I thought I'd go down to Dore's Hardware and buy a new mailbox, but I hadn't yet.

Today's mail was a Kmart flier, an IGA flier, and a square yellow envelope, stiff with the promise of a greeting card. I sighed, not even glancing at the return address before thrusting the thing into my pocket. My sister, the white sheep, ever efficient. The woman *could not* forget a birthday.

I shoved the hatch up until it was more or less closed, and headed down the drive.

Jasper met me in the kitchen with a strident "Now!"

Obediently, I refilled his food bowl; ran water and gave him fresh, glancing over to the window desk as I straightened.

In Aunt Jen's time, the broad plank shelf in the east window had been an indoor herb garden. In this Jen's time it was Communications Central, and held slots for incoming and outgoing mail, a couple pads of paper, some pens, envelopes, a book of stamps, a phone, and an answering machine.

The message-waiting light was blinking.

While Jasper inspected his replenished rations, I hit the replay.

"It's Marian," I told Jasper, who flicked his ear and continued inhaling the contents of his water bowl. Honestly, you'd think I watered the cat on alternate Thursdays.

"Jennifer," the tape announced in a young and painfully formal voice, "this is Marian Younger. I heard on the scanner that Reverend Stern was being transported to Waterville Hospital, and that he's DOA." There was a pause. "I thought you'd like to know. For the paper." Another pause, then a brusque, "Bye."

"Thanks, kid." I tapped rewind and considered the best way to proceed. Tempting as it was to stay home and write my story in the comfort of my own software, common sense dictated a journey to the newsroom and a session with Karen's Computer. There was film to develop, after all, and the background I was going to need on Butchie Stern's life and times could only be found in the groaning file drawers of the *Voice's* morgue.

"I'm going out," I told Jasper, who actually turned his head to look at me. "I might be late." He turned back to his meal.

"I'll miss you, too, okay?" I said and went, across the kitchen and down the ell, to the barn where the Camaro was waiting.

***

THE *WIMSY VOICE* is peaceful on Friday
afternoon. Advertising was dark, both reps "on the road,"
a euphemism for "started Saturday early." Classified
deadline had closed half-an-hour ago, and the phone reps
were on the loose, coffee cups in hand, telling over
weekend plans. Even the business office looked less frantic
than usual— Violet the receptionist actually waved at me
as I went by.

Upstairs, it was twilight. Jack-the-Jock, assistant
sports editor, gave me a nod as I passed his bullpen and I
heard laughter from beyond the movable wall that kept
Features quarantined, away from "working news."

News-side was dark; the scanner over Bill Jacques'
desk was silent. I stopped and flicked it on. Theoretically,
it was never to be off, but Features— or "day-side," as they
referred to themselves— hated the noise and canned the
scanner the minute they hit the deck. It drove Bill Jacques
crazy. But then, Bill Jacques called day-side "the ladies aid
and social society."

I dropped my stuff on Karen's Desk and went back
to the darkroom. I'd only recently been elevated to the
position of Desperate Need Film Tech. Dan Skat allowed
as how he'd taught me all I could learn, which was enough
to get a roll of film developed, if there was no one else
around. Standing orders were: "Don't try anything fancy.
Don't try any burns. Don't do anything cute with the
time. Just do it the way I showed you. And if there's
anybody else here who knows the darkroom, give the film
to them."

I went around the corner, past Dan's cubby, ducking under the silver umbrella. At the end of the short hallway, the darkroom's door stood half open, pale light leaking into the dimness.

Nanci the day-side photographer looked up from the sink and smiled as I poked my head around the door.

"Hi, Jen, what's new?"

"Gloom, doom and destruction," I announced, in my best Boris Karloff, which isn't all that good. Nanci laughed anyway. Nanci laughs a lot.

"You going to be a while?" I asked when she'd reduced her appreciation to a smile. "I've got a couple rolls to do."

She held out a bird-sized hand. "I'll do them. It'll keep me busy while I'm waiting for the shots from the game."

I blinked. "You're working tonight?"

She fluttered her hand. "Big game. Big, *big* game. According to Jack. Mort's shooting."

That explained Nanci's presence. Mort was a freelancer and a sports freak equal to Jack-the-Jock. A decent enough photographer in general, and sometimes inspired in the pursuit of his passion, he was banned from Dan Skat's darkroom. I'd asked why, when I first came to the *Voice,* but people just shook their heads and looked aside. I hadn't quite worked up the nerve to ask Dan.

"Need all of it?" Nanci asked, as I dropped the cans in her palm.

"Please."

"No problem. I'll leave them on your desk."

"I'll be here," I told her, and shivered suddenly in the closed space. "Got a story to write."

"Okay," Nanci said uncuriously and I retreated, back down the hall to my desk.

***

I TURNED ON KAREN'S Computer, pulled out
my notebook and flipped through the pages, circling the
good bits, then numbering them— a kind of on-the-fly
outline. By the time I'd finished, Karen's Computer was up
and panting for action. I chose "1" for "Write"— and dove
in.

Shortly after I found my lead, day-side went noisily
home, plunging the front of the floor into a darkness in
which Jack-the-Jock's desk lamp was the only oasis of light.

The scanner babbled and blared over Bill Jacques'
empty desk: I cocked an ear toward it, trusting my
subconscious to sort the usual cop-and-rescue chatter and
only nudge me for something out of the ordinary.

My fingers worked the keys; the story flowed,
taking on shape and substance, very nearly writing itself.

Somewhere in the time of writing, a stack of black-
and-white photos appeared on the desk: Nanci had come by
without my noticing.

At long last, I reached the end of what I knew of my
own knowledge, what I had witnessed with my own eyes
and heard with my own ears. I saved the file and got up
slowly, wincing as my shoulder snarled spitefully to life,
and walked across the hall to the morgue.

***

BUTCHIE STERN'S FULL and proper handle was
Hyannis Merton Stern III and despite the fact that he had
four sons among his nine living children, there was no
Hyannis Merton the Fourth.

His wife's— his widow's— name was Jacqueline,

formerly Thibeau. Old money. Baptist, which was where Butchie's Reverend derived. Some years back, though, he apparently took exception to the Baptist party line and went off to found his own sort.

Unfortunately, Butchie's sort hadn't seemed to be many other folks' sort and the Church of the Righteous Crusader shut its doors forever barely a year after they had opened. Which was when Butchie took up his cause against "abortionaries."

I filtered it, filled in facts, closed. Went back to the top of the file and started tightening.

# 8

IT WAS TEN BY THE newsroom clock when I shut down Karen's Computer and shrugged into my coat. Jack-the-Jock had his back to me, receiver cradled between shoulder and cheek, fingers banging his keyboard.

A goodbye would have distracted him. I didn't call one.

Down the stairs, out the door, across the nearly-empty lot. The sky was midnight-glittered velvet, lit by a full yellow moon.

I unlocked the Camaro and slid into the driver's seat; touched the ignition and heard the engine spring to life. I pulled the seatbelt snug and leaned back in the seat; staring through the sunroof at the stars, the sky, the moon. Vaguely, I wondered if the Ash's barn was finished. I felt drained, unfocused, but not tired. Not tired— restless.

Eager to run.

The car enclosed me, expectant. I smiled up at the moon and reached down to the stick; slipped it into drive.

We threaded through Wimsy downtown like a panther pacing a doe. At the edge of town, I gunned her.

I reached down, twisted the stereo on, and up. Warren Zevon was singing "Werewolves of London," and I joined in.

The tired lights at the Buckshot Inn came up on the right while Warren and I were howling our second "arooo" and before we'd hit the fourth a classic red Daytona, ram scoop and white wall tires, spun gravel out of the lot, cutting me off as it swung into a left turn so wide it looked accidental.

I bit off in mid-howl, hit brakes, horn, and simultaneously flipped the International Peace Sign toward the other car as it roared past.

"Stupid rednecks," I muttered, taking my foot off the brake and giving the Camaro its head. Warren was still singing, but I was trying to place the car. There were a couple classic autos in and around Wimsy, but they were coddled machines, housed in heated garages and brought out on display a few times during the summer— for a parade or two, maybe, and a couple leisurely drives. The owners were more likely to risk a favorite offspring than chance a scratch on the Classic by taking it out to a dive like the Buckshot— and no one I could think of local owned a red Daytona.

"Should've gotten the license plate, Jen," I told myself. "Some reporter you are."

On the radio, Warren finished his last howl. I glanced in the mirror, expecting to see nothing but dark road and the diminishing lights of the Buckshot behind me.

What I saw instead was— headlights.

Rapidly gaining headlights.

Intuition is a wonderful thing. I barely had time to say "Shit" before my foot was pressing the gas pedal.

The Camaro leapt forward, eager. Behind me, the headlights continued to gain.

I slowed, fractionally, made the turn into Bridge Street without resorting to automatic signals and rolled smartly toward the double line of vapor lights that illuminated the approach to the Waterville bridge, leaned down and snapped the radio off.

Intuition's all very well, I told myself sternly, but the wise reporter makes sure she's actually being followed before she panics.

In the mirror, the dark bulk of a car turned into Bridge Street. I sailed under the first pair of lights and onto the bridge itself, stringently keeping to 45 mph amid the pinkish glow of the vapor lights.

Halfway across the bridge, I looked in the mirror again. The car behind me had passed the second pair of lights: a classic red Daytona, ram scoop, and by no means dallying, sporting Massachusetts tags.

"Shit," I said again and hit the gas.

The Camaro surged forward, leapt off the end of the bridge, flying across the Division's tangle of track. We flew down River Street to the Winslow town line and took the right onto Route 201 without kicking up a nub of gravel, which was fortunate, since a thrown pebble might have nicked the Daytona's windshield. The speedometer read 55.

Winslow had turned off the stoplights on Bay Street for the night. I eased down on the gas, saw the speedometer climb toward 60 as we shot past dark stores and shuttered houses, toward Vassalboro and points more-or-less south, the Massachusetts Daytona right on my tail.

Maine holds a lot of wilderness inside its 33,265 square miles, and only about a million-and-a-quarter people. Massachusetts, a state one-quarter the size, is home to six million. Many Massachusetts residents come north during the year to sample Maine's considerable outdoor pleasures; alas, they are not universally loved by the natives.

"They get up here and see all this empty space," says Harry Pelletier, "and it kicks their common sense all to hell. It ain't meanness so much as ignorance."

But some of it *is* meanness, especially when you're talking in terms of a car full of young men, fresh from a dive which has been known to forget to check IDs, driving Daddy's go-fast car and maybe just a little bored with the Maine night life.

I counted five heads in the mirror and cussed. Wimsy, Waterville and Winslow had local police stations, but I was past them all. I thought about turning up the China Road, going across the Garland Road and doubling back through Benton to the Winslow cop shop, then let the idea go. The Garland Road followed a ridge along the Kennebec; it offered no opportunity for me to lose my pursuers and ample opportunity for the boys to force me off into a ditch, if they decided to get cute.

I hurtled through the China Road intersection, pressing the pedal as I climbed out of Winslow. The Daytona lost a few lengths going uphill and I bore down on the gas. The speedometer hit 70 as I whipped past Pine View Mobile Homes and kissed 75 as I topped the next hill.

Route 201 between Winslow and Augusta invites casual speeding— wide, sweeping curves and good flat straights— and I'd often taken advantage of the road, the hour and the car to indulge myself. Tonight would have been a perfect night for a run, and I'd been looking forward to a moonlit race with myself, but the Daytona changed all that.

They were close again in the mirror, half over the line, taking the curves mushily— an inexperienced driver, or a tired driver, or a drunk driver.

I could take advantage of any of those conditions— or all of them, I thought, and once more pressed the gas.

Obedient, the Camaro surged forward. The Daytona hesitated, then rushed, closing the gap between us dangerously.

I took my bearings: I'd passed Oak Grove a few minutes ago, its towers shining in the moonlight. The Bog

Road was coming up, a hard left into a narrow country lane. I blessed the moon, eased up just a touch on the gas.

Behind me, the driver of the Daytona hit the horn. My eyes leapt to the mirror, saw him giving me the finger, and eased off the gas some more, wondering if that was all they had wanted— chase the girl and scare her, give back what they'd gotten and then let up.

I slowed more. The Daytona didn't. The Camaro jolted; I fought the wheel, turned the skid into a turn, fishtailing into the Bog Road in a swirl of road grit that hung behind me like a silver cloud in the moonlight, shredded as the Daytona roared through.

The posted limit on the Bog Road is 45. I'd recommend 35, unless the day is exceptionally fine, and closer to 25 on a dark night. Better yet, put off your errand 'til daylight.

I was doing 50 before I cleared the first hill, 55 through the first narrow, ill-wished corkscrew turn. The Daytona misjudged the height of the hill and sparks flew when the underside scraped asphalt. It managed to keep focused through the curve, which was good, since the Bog Road really does border a bog, and there's precious little in the way of shoulder.

The second corkscrew almost caught the Camaro, but a quick twist of the wheel saved the day. The Daytona didn't even stutter. Maybe the boys were getting into the challenge of the thing.

Cool.

Another hill and two more corkscrews, with the Daytona keeping right up, and it was beginning to look like this hadn't been one of my better ideas. Then I saw the gap on the right and grinned.

"All right, kids, try this."

Make no mistake, the Bog Road is nasty. But the Old Pond Road is bitter.

I commended my soul to whichever deity had duty this evening and pushed the Camaro up the first incline, through the dog-leg, twist, down, up, right-left— behind me, I heard a large noise.

Cautiously, I eased up on the gas and looked in the mirror.

No Daytona.

The imperatives of the road demanded my attention. I gave it, slowing further, and a couple dog-legs and cat-tail crowded hillocks later looked in the mirror again.

No Daytona.

I grinned, slowed further, and negotiated my way with due respect along to Hanniford Hill, passing the temptation to take dirt-paved Fire Road Three, which came back to 201 about half-a-mile upstream.

Cautiously, driving like a respectable citizen, I turned onto the blacktop at Hanniford Hill, proceeding at a stately 35 mph toward Route 201. I looked up at the mirror— and swore.

Headlights— moving fast.

I gave the Camaro gas, the speedometer climbed to 45 and the headlights behind me grew.

I topped a small rise, saw the blue lights at the bottom of the road and touched the brakes, pulling over to the side. Behind me the Daytona showed no inclination to slow. I hit the horn, slowed more and the Daytona whipped by, one set of wheels in the field, picking up speed.

They skidded around the cop car, taking a left onto 201, back end swinging wide, gunning it. I crept forward and stopped a couple feet from the cop car, rolled down my window and waited while the cop— Winslow cop— walked up to the Camaro, sliding her radio back into its belt-loop.

"Jen." She touched her hat— Officer Mary Goodine. Mary'd been the police force for a town called Larone, before Larone voted itself out of a police force and Mary out of a job. I'd followed her around on her last day, on behalf of the *Voice*— the day when she'd been called upon to break up a domestic quarrel, give a kid caught shoplifting a stern talking-to, write three traffic tickets and one warning and shoot a deer that had been wounded in a collision with a car.

"Mary," I said. "Good to see you."

"Same," she said, pulling out her pad. "Nice night for a drive. Always like to drive when there's a moon." She took the pen out of her breast pocket. I sighed.

"How long them fellas been chasing you?"

"They cut me off in front of the Buckshot," I said. "I blew the horn and gave them the finger and they turned around to argue about it."

Mary nodded. "Got a call from Peasey. He'd gone in to the store because the new alarm system went off. Just leaving when he saw two cars roaring down Bay Street— thought the black car was you, but didn't place the red one." She flipped the pad open.

"Where you headed?"

"Freeport," I said, silently blessing Jim Peasey. "It's my birthday and I wanted to do some shopping at Bean's."

"Can't argue with that," Mary allowed, and the radio on her belt squawked. "'scuse me." She pulled it loose, hit the stud, "Goodine," released the stud and listened to the scratchy, fizzy report.

Long months of listening to the newsroom scanner helped me sort it out. The Daytona had blasted into Augusta, arriving at the rotary to find it blocked at every spoke by a police car. They stopped, had the boys— five boys, between 18 and 20— which was wise of them. The officers had found open containers, the radio reported, and a substance that appeared to be marijuana.

Mary signed off, slid the radio home and looked down at me.

"Spend the night in jail, wake up with a headache and get bailed out by daddy in the morning." She shrugged. "Could've been worse. Might still be worse, if you want to file a complaint. They threaten you? Hurt you?"

I thought about the nudge they'd given the Camaro, then shook my head. If the "substance" *was* marijuana, the cops would confiscate the car, among other things.

"I'm okay," I told Mary.

"Okay." She uncapped the pen and wrote in the pad. My heart sank. A speeding ticket at the level of speed I'd been traveling was going to be serious. By the grace of God, I didn't have any points against my record, but 75 in a 45 mile zone would take care of that, all right. Not that the fine would be trivial....

Mary finished writing and capped her pen.

"Freeport," she said, musingly. "I reckon that's what— about an hour from here?"

It was if you obeyed the speed limits all the way down. I nodded.

"About that," I told Mary.

"That's what I thought." She ripped the page out of the pad. "All right, Jen, you go on and have a nice drive. This is a warning for exceeding the posted limit." She handed me the page and I took it with a blink. "You be careful now. Roads're full of damn fools who don't think the law's about them."

"Thank you," I managed. "I'll be careful."

Mary nodded. "You might want to think about getting

one of them cell-phones. Next time you're in trouble, you can just call the cops."

"I'll think about that." I folded the warning carefully and slipped it into my pocket. "Thanks again, Mary."

"All in a night's work. Evening." She touched her hat and walked back to her car.

Breathing a sigh of relief, I put the Camaro into drive and eased down the Hanniford Hill Road to Route 201, waited for the Winslow police car to clear the intersection, then made a left hand turn onto 201 and continued south, at a sedate and grandmotherly 45 mph.

# 9

FORTY OR SO MILES beyond Augusta, on the Harraseeket River, lies the Town of Freeport.

Whether Freeport had in the past been a free-duty port, I don't know. My interest in the place is economic, not historical. Because, whatever it *had* been, Freeport was now an official Tourist Trap, one of those "restored" towns featuring high-end outlet stores, craft stores, jewelry stores, fast-food restaurants, B&Bs—

And L.L. Bean.

The L.L. Bean Company store in Freeport, Maine, is open for business 24 hours a day, 365 days a year. Within its hallowed walls is contained every item featured in Bean's famous catalog, as well as many that should be, but aren't. It's Mecca to a shopping fool—and a sweet breath of nostalgia to natives of cities where restaurants, gas stations, grocery, video record and liquor stores stay open round the clock.

Gently, I guided the Camaro into a parking slot, killed the engine, got out and locked the door. I felt rested, focused and confident, as I walked down the wide pavement, through the doors that were never locked and into Bean Country, pausing in the lobby to sign the guest book and make certain of my plastic.

Credit cards at the ready, I squared my shoulders and waded into the thick of it.

To do Bean's right would take days. I gave it my best shot, which was three hours. At first, I prowled: picked things up, put things down, leafed through books, played with puppets. At the knife counter, I succumbed to a genuine Swiss Army penknife (*without* the eating utensils) to replace the little pearl-handled orange-peeler I'd been carrying in my pocketbook.

"Happy birthday," I told myself, and slipped the knife away with a flourish.

Feeling like a Real Mainer, I went back up to the children's balcony and pulled the two-foot-tall, anorak-clad, backpack-toting "Bean Bear" down from its high shelf. The Shopping had begun.

\*\*\*

DAWN WAS PINKING the horizon when the Camaro slid into the top of the drive. Slight as the rise was, I could see the Smoke, down behind the trees, boiling its kettle of morning fog. Then the drive twisted down and all I saw was trees.

I left the car in the barn with my loot locked inside, went up the ell and into the kitchen. Jasper blinked at me from the center of the table.

"Hey," I said, mildly.

His eyes widened. Deliberately, because he wanted to, he rose, stretched and jumped lightly from forbidden territory to the floor. A moment later, he levitated into the east window, nimbly avoiding Communications Central, settled in, back to me, and began to wash his face.

I shook my head and hung my jacket on its peg.

"'Night, Jasper," I said, and went upstairs to bed.

\*\*\*

IT WAS PRECISELY eleven o'clock by the brass windup clock when I rose, showered, pulled on jeans, red denim shirt, socks, sneakers— and descended the stairs, ready to face what was left of Saturday.

I unloaded the Camaro while my coffee dripped; drank it while snipping price tags with my shiny new penknife. Slipping the knife away, I shrugged into my jacket, making sure my wallet and keys were in the pocket.

I put down food and clean water for Jasper, who was not in evidence, tucked Bean Bear under one arm and headed down the ell.

Marian Younger lives at the *other* end of Wimsy, on the border of Kennebec and Somerset counties. The house sits tall, crowning a rise from which all vegetation over two inches high has been banished. Plush green stretches in every direction, down to the banks of the Smoke. On a clear day, which this was, you can see the Rangeley mountains, fifty crow-miles beyond the west-facing windows.

I pulled in between Janice's Volvo and Tim's Saab. Bear riding my hip, I went up the four granite steps and pushed the lighted ivory plate in the center of the front door.

Inside, chimes chimed, electronically flawless. The sound faded and I stood, bear on hip, October sun warming my back through two layers of denim.

I'd just made up my mind to ring again, when the door swung soundlessly back, and Timothy Younger, Ph.D., smiled down at me from his lanky six-feet-two.

"Ah, Ms. Pierce. How are you today?" he inquired, precisely as if I were one of the rich-kid students he dealt with daily.

Tim Younger was Dean of Students at Colby, an upscale, very exclusive liberal arts college over in Waterville. He was a decent enough man— a professor, virtually indistinguishable from all the others I'd known throughout my checkered career. I preferred him to his wife, but that was the best I could muster.

"I'm fine, thank you, Dr. Younger," I said, with a smile as bland as his own. "Is Marian at home?"

Now, there was a stupid question. If Marian wasn't at school— and she wasn't, it being Saturday— she was at home. *QED.*

Tim Younger apparently detected no sarcasm in the query. He inclined his head formally.

"In fact, she is." He pulled the door wider and stepped back into the ceramic tiled foyer.

Holding Bean Bear tight to my hip, I crossed the threshold.

"She's in her room," Marian's father told me. "I believe you know the way?"

"Thank you." I left him to close the door by himself and went across the foyer, sneakers gritting against the tiles.

The stairs were covered in thick, wheat-colored carpet. My sneakers made no sound; no lax floorboard cried out under my weight. I stayed to the right, my hand on the smooth cherry banister, avoiding the metal rail next to the wall, where the chair lift ran.

Marian's door was closed. Naturally. I could hear the scanner grumbling as I rapped gently on the fire-proof door.

"Who is it?"

An interesting question from an only child, living alone with her parents.

"Jen."

There was a slight pause. "Enter," Marian said. I turned the knob and went in.

Marian's room is actually a suite. *Marian's quarters* is how I think of it. The first room is small: wide enough for her to turn the chair; I could cross it in a stride— and did, following the scanner babble into the place where Marian lives.

The second room in the suite widens naturally out of the tiny entry hall. The floor is parquet; a ledge about twenty inches above it encircles the space, except where the sliding glass doors give onto the balcony. Parts of the ledge pull out, other parts pull down, some open and close.

The ledge itself is covered with *things*, mostly electronic; each a project in some stage of completion. Under the ledge are cubbies and shelves.

Over the ledge are more shelves; I can reach the top one, but I have to stretch for it. A telescoping gripper leans handy against the desk, in case Marian needs to retrieve a book from the staggering number of volumes in residence. Here and there a stuffed bear reclines, one of the few indications that this is not a white room in a electronics factory.

The other indication sat behind her specially-made desk, fingers moving over the keypad, head angled down, eyes on the screen set below the shiny mahogany surface.

Marian Younger will be thirteen years old on New Year's Day. She has a crisp, glossy cap of black hair and a pair of enormous agate-green eyes. Her hands are wiry, clever and capable. Her face is ivory-toned; her features delicate. Hard lines frame a pale pink mouth that holds nothing of childish softness. There are blue shadows, always, under the gray-green eyes.

Behind me, the scanner squawked, and a man's voice grated something about leaving the car. Marian didn't look up.

"I'm nearly done," she said.

I nodded, settled Bean Bear on the throne-sized leather side chair, shrugged out of my jacket and flung it over the back. The scanner let go with an ear-splitting hoot— the alert code for Wimsy Rescue. I wandered over to the bookshelves, squinting to see some of the higher titles.

Marian's taste in fiction runs to gadget sci-fi and techno-thrillers; fully half of her library is technical, mostly design manuals and software documentation. Occasionally, you'll come across an oddity: a disintegrating copy of *The Secret Garden*, an out-of-date Brownie handbook, a ratty boxed set of the *Lord of the Rings Trilogy* and a leather-bound copy of *The Hobbit*, pages edged in gold.

"Okay," Marian said behind me, and I turned away from the books; walked back to the side-chair and perched on the arm.

She looked up, face a little paler than usual, the circles under her eyes a little darker. "There's a new board."

"There's always a new board," I pointed out. "Where's this one, Mars?"

"Right here. In Wimsy." She dragged a piece of paper toward her, scribbled on it and pushed it across the desk, an almost-smile tugging at her hard, grown-up mouth.

I snagged the note and glanced at it. "Random Access?"

"That's right. Take a look and let me know what you think."

I'd met Marian Younger on a bulletin board— a bizarre little net out of Memphis called *Creature Feature*. We'd exchanged messages for weeks before we discovered that we not only lived in the same state, but in the same *town*.

It was her youth that surprised me, when we finally met face-to-face, not the wheelchair. On some level, I think I'd expected the chair.

Riding computer bulletin boards may seem like a

stupid way to waste valuable time to most busy, grown-up people. But to someone like Marian, chained to a chair and apt to die young of the disease that put her there, the bulletin boards are— however temporary and ephemeral— a way *out*.

I tucked the note into my jeans pocket and glanced up.

"Thanks for the call yesterday on Reverend Stern," I said. "Always need an ear out." I grinned. "Since I can't always be right on the scene."

A flicker of interest showed in the light eyes. "You saw him die?"

"Bloodthirsty, aren't you? No, I am sorry to report that I did not see him die. I only verified that he was dead."

"Verified." For a wonder, her interest intensified. She leaned forward and put her elbows on the desk. "Tell me."

So, I told her about the Ash's barn-raising and Butchie hanging around trying to put the Evil Eye on everyone and shame them into going home and about Scott charging around the barn, white as if he'd been a ghost, instead of maybe seeing one. And me rushing on in like a certified fool, then Bruce Gagnon and the Rescue and how everyone'd gone back to work.

Marian sat like an upscale ivory mannequin, nodding once when the tale was through and I finally shut up.

"That was pretty good— the thing with the filter," she said, and I blinked, absurdly pleased.

"Reading too many cheap murder mysteries," I said, to cover my pleasure. "Anyhow, now maybe we can have a rest from the dead baby marches and the righteous rhetoric on the letters page." I reached behind me and picked up Bean Bear.

"Brought you a present," I said, leaning over and standing the toy on the desk. "Think he'll fit in?"

For a long moment, she didn't say anything, just sat and stared at the bear in his bright red anorak. Then she looked up and I saw two spots of color, almost the shade of the bear's jacket, riding high on each cheek.

"Why are you giving me a present?" she said then, and her voice was harsh.

Anger, and on such a scale— it didn't make sense. And, then, suddenly, it did. In Marian's world, presents were given by condescending adults— the ones who lied to her and gave her no ease from the pain. The ones who pretended that she was— that she could be— only a little girl.

*We* were equals, above the games of deceit and pity. Or we had been.

"Why?" Marian demanded, hands fisted on the arms of the chair.

I met her eyes. "Because it's my birthday."

Hesitation showed. "Really?"

"Yes, really." I sighed in counterfeit annoyance. "Honestly, Marian, get a grip."

"Well, I didn't— " She leaned forward to grasp the bear and pulled him onto her lap. "He's great," she said, head bent over the bear's. She cleared her throat. "Just like Bilbo, right?"

Bilbo Baggins, that would be— of Hobbit fame. Hobbits give presents on their birthdays and get presents on everyone else's birthday, a system that has always struck me as far more reasonable than our own.

"You will have noticed," I told her austerely, "the large furry feet."

She choked a little— it might have been a laugh—and looked up. "How old are you?"

"Thirty-five," I said and waggled my eyebrows. "An old broad. A fossil. A hag."

"Not a hag," she corrected seriously. "Hags aren't 'til

menopause."

I swallowed. "What have you been reading *now?*"

"For school," she said righteously. "We're studying ancient goddess religions. Ancient goddess religions," she confided, glancing down at the bear in her lap, "are very in."

I laughed and got to my feet. "They are that. Need anything in town?" This, I was allowed to ask; equals could do favors for each other. Besides, I owed her one for yesterday's call.

"No, thanks," she said, her hand on the bear's head, her eyes serious and green.

"Okay, then. I'll let you know what I think about this new board. See you around." I snagged my jacket and turned to go.

"See you around, Jen," Marian said softly, and then, even softer: "Thanks."

## 10

I'D FINISHED STOWING the groceries and was folding the last bag for storage in the pantry when I heard a vehicle coming down the drive.

Jasper streaked across the kitchen floor and leapt into the window over the sink. I stayed where I was, smoothing the bag and listening.

It was definitely a car— not Harry's rattletrap truck, or Morris' more mannerly pickup. Quiet, but with a nearly subaural growl of power— I dropped the bag to the table on my way past and hit the porch just as the Kennebec County Sheriff Department's khaki Lumina pulled into my dooryard and stopped.

Bruce Gagnon got out. He was in full uniform, right down to the Colt clipped on his belt, and he wasn't smiling.

"Afternoon, Sheriff," I called, just like a real Mainer, and stepped to the edge of the porch. "Pretty day, isn't it?"

Bruce didn't answer until he got to the bottom of the three-step flight. He braced his foot on the second step and looked up at me, face serious in the shadow of his hat brim.

"Afternoon, Jennifer," he said then. "Mind if I come in?"

Don't get me wrong: I am not a cop-hater. My grandfather'd walked a beat, back when a cop could walk Mulberry Street and live. My uncle is still a cop— Maryland State Smokey. My dealings with Bruce Gagnon had always been cordial.

So, it must have been sheer contrariness that made me open my mouth and blurt, "Why?"

He used a forefinger to push his brim up about a millimeter.

"I've got a couple questions," he said.

"About what?" I heard myself ask in a frosty imitation of calm.

"About yesterday afternoon," Bruce answered. I shivered a little in the cooling air, then went back a step and pulled open the door.

"Come on in."

Bruce was up the steps and across the porch in two long strides. He hesitated for a second on the threshold, sending a quick, cop-look into my face, then stepped into the kitchen ahead of me.

I followed, letting the door bang shut. There was a *thud!* that was Jasper hitting the floor from the window above the sink. Over Bruce's shoulder I saw him stalk off into the dining room, tail straight out behind him.

"Glass of cider?" I asked, moving to the refrigerator.

"No, thank you," said Bruce as my hand touched the latch. I opened the door anyway and pulled out the jug. I carried it to the counter, opened a cabinet and got down a rocks glass.

"So," I said as I poured, "you've got a couple questions about yesterday. Like what?"

"Like," Bruce said quietly as I capped the jug and started back toward the fridge, "what were you doing at the Ash's?"

I turned my head to stare at him. He stared back, a broad-shouldered middle-aged guy in a crisp khaki uniform. It struck me that he looked tired, even off-color. I put the cider away and shut the door.

"I was doing a story about the barn-raising," I said.

He nodded. "So the paper sent you."

"No," I said grumpily, "the paper didn't send me. It was a command performance— Harry wanted to gloat and wanted someone with her while she did. I figured if I had to go to the damn' thing I might as well get paid, so I brought along the extra camera, grabbed some shots— talked to some people." I shrugged.

"I should have thought of it myself— nice, upbeat follow to Thursday night's meeting...." I trailed off, seeing, with all the force of a very powerful imagination, Butchie Stern lying dead on the dead grass, tie bunched under his chin.

"Right." Bruce leaned a hip against the table and pulled out his notebook. "Why don't you tell me what you saw?"

"What I *saw?*" I went back to the counter, picked up the glass and drank. Sweetness pierced my tongue and I put the glass down with a thump, glaring at Bruce through an abrupt wash of tears.

"What I saw *when?*"

"You were with the body when I arrived," he pointed out mildly. "I wonder how you got there, what things were like when you arrived— like that."

We'd been through all that, just briefly, while we waited for Wimsy Rescue. But Bruce was a cop and I was the granddaughter of a cop. Cops always ask twice. They can't help themselves.

So I didn't point out that we'd already had this talk, and did tell him, once more, for old time's sake, how I'd happened to be at Butchie's side, and him no longer breathing.

He listened close, beginning to end, every now and down jotting something down in his book. When I was finished, he nodded and was quiet for a minute or so, flipping the pages back and forth. I reached for my glass and finished the cider— carefully.

"Okay," Bruce said suddenly. "Now, you stated that Scott Ash came running around the corner of the barn, toward the house and away from the location of the body by the hayrolls, correct?"

Except that I hadn't known there was a body by the hayrolls. I frowned, but gave the man his answer.

"Correct."

"How did he look?"

"Scott? He looked scared out of his mind."

"In what way, particularly?" Bruce wanted to know.

I sighed. "His face was pale, he was panting, he was running hard and whatever he was running from had disturbed him so much that he passed within six inches of me and never turned his head."

"Okay," Bruce said, noting notes. "Okay." He looked up, meeting my eye. "You're a good observer," he said, candid-like; "notice a lot of things. Think back and see if you remember whether he was carrying anything."

I blinked."Carrying— "

"Take your time and think back," he urged.

He seemed to expect some sort of show, so I closed my eyes and found that I *was* thinking back: there I was, and there was the barn and there was Craig behind me, calling "Hey..."— and then the sound of someone pounding across the dead grass and my back against the scrubby barn-siding and Scott flying around the corner, elbows pumping, face pasty and damp....

"He didn't have anything in his hands," I said, and

opened my eyes.

Bruce frowned, looked down and made a note. "You're sure," he stated, not looking up.

"I'm sure."

"Okay." He flipped the book closed and straightened. "Kind of funny," he said then, "man goes running by you, scared blind— and you run *back* the way he'd come. Why was that?"

I pushed away from the counter and met his eyes. "I'm an idiot," I told him, with total sincerity, then, before he could find his line, pitched one of my own.

"What is all this anyway, Sheriff?"

He frowned, not sure whether he was going to tell me, then shrugged. "Investigation into the death of Reverend Hyannis Stern."

"What's to investigate? Everybody knew he had a bad heart."

He glanced aside while he stowed notebook and pen, and I abruptly *knew* what the questions were for.

"You think Scott Ash *killed* Butchie Stern?" I demanded, leaning forward and staring into his face. "Why?"

He met my eyes. "I'm not able to comment on that right now," he said, straight out of the Rule Book. He reached up to settled his brim, and started across the kitchen.

"Thanks for your time," he said, pausing with his hand on the latch. "You'll be around, won't you? I might need to talk to you again."

I stared at him; cleared my throat. "I'll be around."

"Good." He opened the door, brought two fingers up to the brim in a half-salute. "Take care."

"Right," I said flatly. Bruce sort-of smiled and let

himself out.

I heard him cross the porch. Heard the car's door open, then close. Heard the engine growl to life, then fade up the hill.

When I could no longer hear the engine or the sound of tires on the sparse gravel of the drive, I crossed the kitchen, and locked the door.

\*\*\*

THE PRINTER HUMMED briefly and extruded a page— another. It hummed a second longer and politely turned itself off. So now there was a sidebar for the Death in the Hay story. Bill Jacques would cry real tears.

Not that it was much of a sidebar. I'd drawn a blank with the Medical Examiner's Office— not too surprising of a Saturday evening. That would have to wait for Monday, by which time I ardently hoped it would be proved for all time and to everyone's satisfaction that Butchie'd been done by his own faulty ticker. Then he could lie down and be normally dead. There'd be a funeral, those who'd loved him— there must be someone— would do their mourning and start the process of putting together a life without him.

I reached over the pulled the pages out of the printer.

Then I closed the word processor and invoked the modem, fully intending to call the Net and collect my e-mail. Finger on the switch, I hesitated.

Leaning back in the chair, I fished a rumpled scrap of paper out of my jeans pocket and squinted at Marian's cranky writing.

*Random Access*— and a local phone number.

What the heck.

I entered the number in my dialing log, saved it, then

called it up.

Inside the computer, seven quasi-melodic beeps sounded, followed by the ringing of a telephone on the far side of the line.

A computer picked up on the second ring, its carrier signal a spray of static. My machine identified itself, there was a momentary tonal-tug-of-war, then....

CONNECTED my machine told me jubilantly.

The screen went blank for an instant, then letters began to appear, in stately, deliberate lines...

Welcome
You have reached
RANDOM ACCESS BBS
A place exactly like
No place you've ever been
Your sysop is
Fox

# 11

THERE HAD ONCE BEEN a time, in the first flush of electronic youth, when you or I or anyone else could sign onto a BBS— any BBS— using only a "handle." Thanks to the combined efforts of AT&T, the federal government and out-of-control punk hackers, this is no longer the case. A system operator— or "sysop"— is by law required to run a righteous board. Real names must be given, and real voice phone numbers, so the sysop can verify your existence, your age— and the fact that you, and not your best enemy, signed onto his board.

Big services, like The Net, allow you a handle, *after* you have registered your real name, address, daytime and evening phone— and major credit card number. Small, privately run bulletin boards simply can't take the risk.

It had been a long time— it had been *years*— since I'd been faced with a sysop calling himself (or herself) simply 'Fox', though in my day I'd rubbed electronic shoulders with "god," "Geronimo," "Miss Kitty" and hundreds more.

But times had changed. The only boards that allowed pure handles anymore were the so-called "pirates," where the punk hackers and the troublemakers hung out.

I will have to say that I hesitated, my finger over the disconnect, for a very long moment, indeed.

My curiosity finally won— or the gut-level belief that *no one* was stupid enough to start a pirate board in Wimsy, Maine.

I touched ENTER.

More letters scrolled up the screen; froze in position so that I could read:

*Random Access BBS is a law-abiding citizen. If you have illicit phone or credit card numbers, do not post them here. If you break code and long to strut your stuff, this is not the street for you. If you are a warez dude or a cowboy, you may come in, but you must remove your hat, wear a shirt, and remember to always say please and thank you. In the event these concepts are new to you, a short list is appended.*
 *NO PHREAKING*
 *NO FLAMING*
 *NO HACKING*
 *If you cannot abide by these*
 *conditions, drop carrier NOW.*

My eyebrows had climbed high onto my forehead; I could feel them wriggling there, just below the hairline. This was something a little out of the ordinary, even by Baltimore standards. For Wimsy, it was unprecedented.

Of course, *any* Wimsy BBS was all-but-unprecedented. I touched ENTER.

The standard Fed warning scrolled up, boxed and forbidding, informing me that there was no such thing as "private" electronic mail and that the system operator was required by law to report any misdeeds to the proper authority.

I touched ENTER.

The screen blanked, then bloomed with a bright field of flowers— *Nice graphics* I thought, envious— underlined by a sober row of letters.

*Please tell me your real name: First, Last:*

I obliged and quickly went through a sign-on questionnaire that was remarkable for the gentleness of its questions.

At the end of it, the screen blanked again; reset itself almost immediately.

*Welcome, Jennifer. Your initial security level is 5, which means you may browse the system and leave messages in The Speakeasy. You have 20 minutes allotted today. Enjoy!*

There was a very nice graphic of a fox at the end of this. I spent a minute admiring it before I touched ENTER and was admitted to Random Access.

***

IT WAS A NICE BOARD, honey-smooth and spacious. The social section— The Speakeasy— held about a dozen amiable messages, at least half of them attached to feminine names.

Marian's message was typical— a terse little "Hi, I'm here" that managed to skim past such superfluities as age before leaping into the important stuff.

*Does anyone know where to get the star-shaped screwdriver needed to open the case on the AXER PS-3? I don't have anything remotely like it in my kit.*

I grinned and went on to the next posting.

*Marian, it would help me help you if I knew why you \*need\* to open your computer. Are you simply curious regarding the interior landscape? Or do you suspect there's something amiss within the brain? Tell all.*

Fox.

That was the last message. I considered for a moment, then tapped < E > for Enter a Message, addressed it to "All" and invoked the full-screen editor.

*Hi,* I typed. *I'm glad to see there's finally a BBS local to Wimsy. I grew up on the small social boards and I miss them. You just don't get the same kind of camaraderie on the big services.*

My screen shivered, broke apart— reformed as a plain

blue surface, bisected by a thin white line.

*Hello, Reporter Lady.*

The words formed quickly, surely, beneath the line.

*Fox Here.* Two returns: my signal to reply.

*Hello Fox There*, I returned, feeling a smile at the corner of my mouth as I typed. *Hard to stay incognito in Wimsy.* Two returns.

*Ah, but you're famous!* the words below the line assured me and I heard the whisper of his voice— I was certain Fox was "he" now— inside my head, all ruffly with laughter.

*Right*, I typed. *Flatlander makes good.*

*Now, now*, he chided. *The way I hear it, you're turning the paper around— solid writing, always get the quotes right, always check your facts. \*Not\* what I hear about some others, who should, I suppose, in the interest of good manners, remain nameless.*

I felt my eyebrows wriggling high again. *Voice* insider gossip? My fingers flickered over the keyboard.

*You work at the paper?*

*I? I'm a gadabout, child. No visible means.*

*Nice work*, I commented.

*If you can get it*, he agreed. *How was the barn raising?*

I shivered slightly— How did he— then shook myself. Really, Jennifer, I scolded, that's an easy one.

My fingers in the meantime had been typing; I looked at the screen to see what I'd said.

*You weren't there?*

*Alas. But I hear all the rest of the world dropped by, including my very good friend Hyannis Stern. Did he have a lovely time?*

A block of ice had taken up sudden residence in the pit of my stomach. Butchie Stern had four living sons, any one of whom could be Fox— the black sheep, perhaps, and still ignorant of his father's death. Or Fox could indeed be one of Butchie's oldest and most valued friends— I could have been reading irony where none was intended. Damn my imagination!

*Jennifer?* The screen inquired gently. *What's wrong?*
*I'm sorry,* I typed carefully.
*Reverend Stern is dead. DOA at Waterville Hospital, Friday afternoon.*

I stopped typing, no carriage returns to signal him to reply, and sat with my ears straining, as if I might hear a cry of grief through the computer's speaker.

There was, indeed, an entire minute of silence, when the only words on the screen were the words we had already typed. Then:

*I think I see here that Hyannis Stern is dead,* Fox typed slowly. *Verify?*

I set my fingers to the keys.
*Verified.*

There was another pause, not as long as the first. When he began typing again I had the impression of a sigh.

*How strange life is, to be sure. Can you tell me details?*

I considered, then shrugged. He would read the whole story in Monday morning's paper anyway.

*He apparently just fell over and died by the hay rolls out back of the barn. Scott Ash found him.*

*I see. And the cause of death?*

That was trickier, though still nothing he wouldn't learn by reading.

*He had a bad heart,* I typed. *At first, they thought it was heart failure, but the deputy sheriff was by here this evening, asking questions. *Advising* me not to leave the state.*

*That's friendly,* he commented. *Are you okay?*

I grinned, though it felt wobbly on my face.

*Hey, Bruce isn't going to use the hoses in the first session. Cops always ask questions. It's their job.*

*I bow to the type of authority,* Fox answered and I imagined him formally bowing his head. *Thank you for the information and, as much as I regret it, I see by the clock on the wall that your time has just about expired for the day. It was lovely chatting with you. I do hope I'll see you here again.*

*You will,* I assured him. *Unless, of course, they arrest me.*

*Of course.* Fox agreed courteously, followed by a quick *CYA* — the standard goodbye.

I didn't get a chance to return the farewell; the board took control and logged me, firmly but gently, off.

Nor did they come to arrest me, that night or Sunday.

They arrested Scott Ash instead.

# 12

"HEY, *JENNY*, " MILT was leaning over my computer, elbows propped on the monitor, smarmy smile on his too-pale face.

Let there be no mistake: I do not like Milton Vane. At times, I do not like him to the point of visceral loathing. Most days I simply despise him. This was not most days.

After an initial glance at his face, I kept my eyes on the screen, fingers steadily beating the tired keypad, entering the facts about a blood drive to be held at Wimsy Elementary School on Saturday.

"What?"

"What, *please*," Milt instructed.

I sighed, spaced for the next paragraph and kept typing.

There was a pause while Milt decided which would annoy me more: going away without delivering his news, or forking over.

Forking over won. It almost always did.

"I was just down the cop shop," he muttered, leaning close over the top of the monitor. I felt his breath on my hair. "They arrested your guy."

There is no one in Wimsy, or anywhere else on the planet, who could reasonably be called "my guy," but this doesn't bother Milt. "My guy" is a highly flexible term in his personal lexicon and can mean anyone from the press-boss to a high school kid I'd interviewed about his hobby.

"Which guy?" I inquired tiredly, typing "30" at the end of the brief and saving it. I flipped the page I'd been copying face down and started transcribing the next in the stack.

During the tenure of Barbara and Tilden Rancourt The *Voice* had employed not one, but two, news clerks. The Talbot Twins had immediately cut that luxury in half, then danced merrily when the remaining clerk quit because she couldn't handle the doubled workload. Reporters can enter news briefs in their spare time, The Twins decreed— and it was so.

By rights, Milt should even now be transcribing his own stack of briefs. He wouldn't, though— or only at the last possible minute, with Bill Jacques standing over his desk, metaphorical baseball bat raised high.

"*Which* guy?" Milt repeated, in loud and bogus surprise. "Why, your Scott-guy. Who else?"

My fingers stumbled on the keys. I folded my hands in my lap, pushed my chair back six inches and looked up into Milt's unlovely face.

"On what?"

Milt giggled and rubbed his hands together in unwholesome glee.

"Murder," he said. And giggled again.

\*\*\*

I DROVE OUT TO the Johnson Place, guiding the Camaro carefully down the rutted drive, and parked in the dooryard next to an old blue Escort. I glanced at the refurbished barn as I slid out of the car, squinting at the places where the new siding abutted the old. The neighbors had done a good job: The Ash sheep had a tin-roofed palace to winter in. As I watched, a brown cat came around the corner of the hay-door, orange kitten dangling from her mouth.

I turned and crossed the yard, avoiding bits of scrap

wood, went up to the porch and raised my hand to knock.

The door popped open before my knuckles touched wood and Merry Ash was there, eyes red-rimmed and stormy in a strained white face.

"What the hell do you want?"

I cleared my throat. "To talk to you."

"The *Voice* wants a quote from the wife of the accused?" The question was bitterly sarcastic— and it hurt, enough that I answered in kind.

"I'm on my break, okay?"

Merry blinked, then stepped back, holding the door wide.

"Okay. C'mon in."

I did, sneakers gritting on the ancient linoleum. The kitchen was dim, cool. A scrubbed pine table stood in the middle of the floor, two discount-store wooden chairs pushed neatly to. Clean dishes sat in a drying rack on the counter; the chipped enamel sink gleamed snow-white.

"Have a seat," Merry said, pointing toward the table and its tidy honor guard. "Want a cup of tea?"

"Thanks."

Merry nodded, plucked the red kettle from the stove, ran water into it and swung it back onto the burner. She twisted a knob; I heard the click-click-click of the propane feed, then saw a bright whoosh of blue flame, before she turned back the gas and came to stand in front of me.

She looked bad. If I'd been Wiccan or claimed any sort of Sight, I'd have said I could see the energy fizzing off of her in big yellow and blue sparks.

"You know they arrested Scott," she said all at once. "Stupid cops think he killed Reverend Slime."

"I heard that," I said, trying to keep my voice even and calm.

Unfortunately, I hadn't heard much else. A call to Bruce Gagnon had netted a confirmation that Scott was in custody and a polite, "No comment, sorry," to my other questions.

The State Medical Examiner verified that the death in question was a homicide— period. He recommended I speak with the sheriff's department.

"Nobody'll talk to me," I told Merry. "I gather they've decided it wasn't heart failure, and there's no question of an accident...."

Merry laughed. I think it was a laugh.

"No question of accident," she said, half-wildly. "Oh, no. You've got to know exactly what you're doing for this one. That's why they latched onto Scott— and they're not going to let go...." Her face wavered, then reset, more strained than before. "Oh, Goddess. We came here— it was going to be different. It was going to be *better*...."

"Why exactly did they latch onto Scott, Merry?" I said it as soft as I could. I wasn't sure she'd heard, but—

"Because of the way he died," she said, blinking at me. "Because Scott was in Special Forces— and that's where you learn to kill like that. No place else."

I sat, thinking back over Bruce's polite "no comment" and the medical examiner's impatient "that's all," and looking at Merry Ash, standing before me strained and half-wild— and in possession of information she should not in the general way of things possess.

"How do you know that?" I asked. It came out sharper than I'd intended. Merry's brows pulled together.

"Know what?"

"How Reverend Stern died," I said. "Who told you? The cops?" That really wasn't too likely, but how else...?

Before me, Merry shifted, stood straighter, face going still and stern. Eyes pinning mine, she raised her hand— and made a sign.

I shook my head. "I'm not in the Craft," I said, meaning I was neither a Wiccan nor an associated pagan.

"You've studied," she insisted, eyes still tight on mine. "You knew the sign."

"I studied," I admitted, not quite stifling the sigh. "But I didn't graduate."

She lowered her hand. "I'll tell you. In Circle."

Which means confidential, close enough. What's told in Circle stays in Circle. No matter what.

I nodded. "In Circle. I agree."

"Okay," she said, mouth twisting a little. "One of the EMTs is in Gaia Coven. He noticed the wound when he was getting Reverend Slime ready to defibrillate—in the ambulance."

Gene Warner my brain provided helpfully, showing me a picture of the mustached EMT as I'd last seen him, then showing a quick-clip from the We Are Wimsy Day parade: Gene sporting a "Witches are Crafty Critters" T-shirt, standing with the other coven members in the instant before Butchie Stern walked into Merry Ash. I nodded again— it made sense that Gene would bring that sort of news to Merry. It wasn't especially ethical, but it made sense.

"Right," I said. "So the cops think it was Scott because Butchie died from a Special Forces-style kill and Scott used to be Special Forces."

Reasonable enough of them, really. Except that Scott had been ghost-faced terrified when he passed me on the way from Butchie's body— *not* the sort of reaction one would expect from a Special Forces guy who had just completed a planned murder.

I looked at Merry. I looked at her eyes— *into* her eyes— and took a careful breath.

"So, did Scott kill Reverend Stern?"

She didn't even try to break my gaze. "No," she said flatly, "but I know who did."

The kettle began to scream.

*** 

"THIS HAPPENED A COUPLE years ago— we were in Baltimore, I think...." Merry frowned and stirred a spoonful of honey into her tea.

"Yeah, it was Baltimore. I'd picked up a job stringing for the *City Paper*— Scott was working construction— big job out in the county— a mall, I think. Horrible hours, but it was a Rouse project and no way Scott was going to turn down that kind of money...." She pulled the spoon out of her mug and laid it on the table top.

"So anyhow, he's working these long hours, physical labor, getting four, five hours sleep a night and his edge is starting to go. He feels himself slipping, goes to the shift boss and does the right thing— says he's tired and it could be getting to the point where he might make a mistake. Hurt somebody. Says he'd like the rest of the day off— report back fresh tomorrow." She sighed, shook her head and drank some tea.

"Shift boss didn't buy it. Told Scott the best he could do was give him half-an-hour right now to get his shit in gear. So Scott takes the half-hour, finds himself a corner, sits on the floor with his back to the wall and puts himself under— " She glanced up, eyes questioning.

"I know," I told her.

She nodded— "Right"— and picked the thread up.

"Okay. He's in trance, just floating, thinking about

nothing in particular, and there's a voice. The voice is saying, 'Look at this man and know him.' And Scott's thinking, 'What man?' and the voice gets louder, sort of shouting, and it says, 'Open your eyes and know this man!' And Scott thinks, 'What *is* this?' but he opens his eyes and in front of him there's this guy— big blond guy, rock hero type. And Scott thinks, 'Okay, I'll recognize him, if I see him again' and he closes his eyes, but there's still the voice and it's yammering fit to beat five bands: 'Death follows this one. When you see him again, a man will die.'

"Well, that sounded pretty serious, so Scott opens his eyes again, but the guy's gone. Scott leans his head back against the wall and closes his eyes, trying to figure out what to do now, because he's even tireder than ever and he's only got a couple minutes left to get completely revitalized and ready to work.

"Behind his eyes— that's how he put it— behind his eyes, someone's waiting for him. Scott recognizes him right away, starts to say the name, but the God smiles and reaches down and says, 'Take my hand,' and Scott does." Merry sighed lightly, staring down into her mug.

"The next thing he knew, his shift-boss was shaking him; telling him he'd used up his half-hour and ten minutes more and was he working this shift or was he unemployed? He went back to work, fresh, he said, as if he'd slept eight hours right through. Came home that night and told me all about it, looking better than he had for weeks. At first, we both kept an eye out for big blond guys, but Scott never saw his particular guy again." She raised her eyes to mine.

"Until Friday. The guy you came with— that's him. Scott came and told me as soon as he saw."

I took a careful breath, drawing on years of secretarial expertise to keep my face politely blank. After a moment, I slid my eyes from hers, down to my mug. I picked it up and drank. Set it back in its place and looked up.

"So Scott thinks Craig is the guy he saw in his vision? The guy the God warned him about?"

Relief washed through Merry's eyes. Almost, she seemed to smile. "Right."

"Okay." I closed my eyes and ran back through it, ignoring the voice in the back of my brain that kept shouting that what cops believed in was *evidence*, not visions. Finally, I shook my head and opened my eyes.

"Doesn't fit."

Merry frowned. "Why not?"

"Well, for a couple reasons. First, look at what the God said, that death followed this one and the next time Scott saw him, someone would die. *Not* that Craig was going to kill someone. Right?"

Reluctantly, she nodded. "Right."

"Then there's the matter of a weapon."

Her face changed, going from half-hope to despair in an instant. "Weapon."

I frowned. "The medical examiner said it was murder. Your coven-mate said there was a wound. Therefore, there is a murder weapon."

Wearily, she shook her head. "The weapon you're talking about might be anywhere," she said. And it probably won't ever be found. You wouldn't need much— a hatpin, maybe, or a length of wire. Probably wire, so whoever did it just puts it back in his pocket and strolls away." She swallowed and looked aside.

"As kills go, it's real clean, real fast— barely leaves a trace. You punch the wire about half-an-inch into the solar plexus— that stops the heart. Reverend Slime probably never knew what hit him." She looked at me. "I know that because Scott told me, Okay?"

"Okay," I said softly.

Merry shook her head, face leaden.

"You just have to know where to hit, that's all," she said. "Human beings are really pretty fragile."

# 13

PREMIUM GRADE SUNLIGHT poured out of
the flawless sky, coating everything in thick yellow
radiance. The leaves glowed: red, yellow, orange. Grass was
a heartbreaking, improbable emerald. The sidewalks shone.
Tarmac lustered. Even the Wimsy General Store looked
good, flaked shingles reborn to glory beneath the
benediction of the light.

I drove, staring at October beyond the windshield,
windows up, stereo off, alone and trying to think.

Merry swore Scott hadn't killed Butchie Stern, but I
was pretty sure Merry would swear so— God and
Goddess— if she'd watched Scott do the deed.

Merry also swore that the God Himself had taken
time out of His busy schedule to warn His goodman Scott
of a certain individual known in Other Realms as a
harbinger of death. Scott had been sleep-poor and stressed-
out at the time— metaphysical flypaper for any visions that
happened to flutter close. If you happened to believe in
visions.

I sighed and turned onto River Road. On my right,
the Smoke glittered and flowed, sated with sunlight.

Cops did not believe in visions. Cops believed in
facts, in the murder weapon and in probable cause. Scott
Ash had the knowledge, the opportunity and what some
might think was reason enough.

I considered that last. Reason enough? Man puts
himself in your way at every turn, derides your religion,
calls your wife a whore in all but word at the most-

attended public meeting of the season? That could be reason enough. Who in Wimsy knew Scott Ash well enough to say that it wasn't? Besides himself— and his wife.

I shook my head. Even if the weapon never surfaced, Scott was in bad trouble.

And it had nothing— absolutely and entirely *nothing*— to do with me.

The Camaro cruised over an orgy of track— train track, Division track, switch track— and I touched the brake pedal, eased the wheel right, and drove into the lot for the new public boat landing. The orange paint outlining the parking spaces gleamed like gold.

I killed the engine, pocketed the keys and walked across the emerald grass to the furthermost picnic table. Hoisting myself onto the table, sneakers on the bench, elbows on knees, I stared down into the Smoke.

Scott had not killed Butchie Stern.

I *knew* it.

And it would just be oh-so-helpful if I also *knew* who had.

There'd been dozens of people at the Ash's barn-raising, most of them men, and most, Maine being Maine, holding former rank in one branch or t'other of the United States Armed Forces. It was not too optimistic to assume that there had been retired Special Forces or Green Beret among them.

As for who else might have wished the Reverend mortal harm— that number, alas, was legion.

For Butchie had not been content to merely force his belief system upon the citizens of Maine. My, no. Butchie had traveled— and traveled widely, according to the clips in the *Voice's* morgue.

He'd been in Kansas, doing blockade shifts at Planned

Parenthood clinics. He'd been in Texas. Philadelphia.
Chicago. He'd marched on D.C., leading his own bus-load
of followers down Pennsylvania Avenue.

He'd been arrested a couple times: trespassing.
Disturbing the peace. Terrorizing. Proud wounds, every
one, honorably taken in war.

His name must appear on the hate list of a thousand
women, their sisters, mates or lovers.

But he'd died at home, among his neighbors, one of
whom had hated him bad enough to act.

*Who?*

Two feet away and five feet down, the Smoke ran
lazy and sun-sodden. I rubbed my eyes, bent 'til my
forehead touched my knees and hunched there, listening to
my thoughts yammer.

Scott Ash had not killed Butchie Stern. A trained
killer, having killed, does not then call attention to himself
by running, white-faced and terrified, from the scene of the
crime. Rather, he strolls casually back to the busy crowd,
eases in, picks up a hammer or a saw....

*Knock it off, Jen. Bruce Gagnon isn't going to accept
your interpretation of how seasoned killers act any more than
he's going to accept Scott's vision.*

That stirred something. I sat up, blinking against the
thick light. Scott had been *truly frightened*— not of me, but
of the man with me.

Craig, foretold of the God.

Alone, of all the people there, who had no reason to
dislike, or even know, Hyannis Stern. Fingered as the
omen of death.

Round and round.

And round. And round.

*Your're losing your mind,* I told myself, and

proceeded to tell myself other things: that it was, emphatically, none of my business. That cops do cop work better than anyone. That women who live alone in the boonies, with only a cat and a computer for company, are apt to get a little— strange.

That *I* don't believe in visions— or in any sort of magic, for that matter. Which explains my non-Wiccanhood. I admire the Craft; in many ways it resonates truth within me. But to be a Witch is to believe in magic. And there my brain rebels.

*For God's sake, Jen,* I snarled at myself, *let it be. If Scott's innocent, the cops'll find out. Or a jury of his peers will.*

Except that innocent people went to jail every day, while axe murderers walked free.

I straightened, carefully, and sat there a few minutes longer, kneading my shoulder to unknot the worst of the kinks. That done, I slipped off the bench and walked back to the Camaro, started the engine— and headed home.

*** 

MORRIS' BROWN PICKUP was parked in my dooryard, "Old Smoky Orchard" shining like butter in the sunshine.

Craig was on the steps, arms draped loosely around his knees. The sun kissed him shyly at the edge of porch-shade, investing him with aura like an angel.

In the cocoon of my car, I sighed, nosed in close to the old oak, killed the engine and popped the door.

Craig rose from his seat on the top step and came to meet me, smiling— uncertainly, I thought.

"Hi," he said, hesitating before me. He aimed a glance at my face, but it shied at the last second and took off over my shoulder. He cleared his throat.

"Nice car."

"Thanks," I said, amused in spite of myself. *Rock Legend Just Shy Guy*, the headline-writing portion of my brain supplied helpfully. Bill Jacques never used any of my headlines, naturally, but I kept writing them. Practice makes perfect.

"What can I do for you?" I asked Craig, and this time he managed to look me in the eye.

"Payday," he said, with a genuine grin. "Thought you'd let me buy you a slice of pizza."

I hesitated, reluctant to involve myself in a relationship with a gorgeous, by-definition ego-bloated, hunk. *Or with any other human being*, my brain noted sardonically.

Busy brain, just when I needed one least. Well, what the hell. Craig seemed like a reasonable human being, despite his apparent interest in dating a woman ten to twelve years his senior. He could do much better in town—a lot better if he took himself and his physique to one of the so-called "clubs" in Waterville. Likely, he didn't know that. Likely, I could find a way to clue him in, across the course of a pizza. It'd be the neighborly thing to do.

*Besides*, my brain whispered, *maybe you can find out if he was in Special Forces*.

Sometimes I hate my brain.

"Sure," I said to Craig, and smiled. "Pizza sounds great."

\*\*\*

I DROVE US DOWN TO the Wimsy House of Pizza, where we took over the rear booth, me with my back to the room and Craig with his against the wall. On my advice, he ordered up a veggie-double-cheese— the specialty of the house— and added a pitcher of Coke on his own initiative.

The Coke came and he filled a mug for each of us, then settled back and smiled.

"So, what'd you do today? Cover a bank hold-up?"

"Nobody'd rob the Wimsy Credit Union," I told him. "They wouldn't get their gas money back."

He laughed. "*And* they know it."

I grinned. "Bank knows how to advertise," I said, and felt the grin fade. I looked down into the mug. There were chips of ice floating on the sticky black surface. I poked at them with my straw.

"Bad day?" Craig asked.

I looked up. "Sorry. Yeah, sort of. The cops arrested Scott Ash."

"The guy owns the barn?" Craig frowned and took a swig of soda. "How come?"

I paused, thinking that the God could hardly have chosen a more unlikely messenger of death, then looked close into his eyes.

"Murder."

The blue eyes blinked, the beautiful face registered mild surprise.

"Bummer," he commented, and tipped his head. "Who do they think he killed?"

"Reverend Stern— the man who died at the barn-raising."

Craig appeared to think about that while he finished off the last of his drink and poured another.

"Wasn't that a— whadycallit— a heart attack? That's what they were saying on the crew. Said he'd been in the hospital with the heart in the winter— supposed to take it easy. But he was a busy kind of guy— always going here, going there, getting himself all fired up over these clinics or whatever it was." Craig drank some more soda.

"I guess everybody thought that at first," I said carefully. "But they think different now." I sighed. "I talked to the medical examiner. He said homicide, no question."

"Wow." Craig didn't sound particularly impressed. He looked at me and grinned. "Come to Maine," he said, "and get away from it all."

"The way life should be," I agreed, quoting the latest tourism department tagline. I sighed. "I went to see Merry— Scott's wife. She's pretty upset."

"Yeah, well, I guess she would be," Craig allowed vaguely.

At which point the pizza arrived.

The business of balancing and devouring sauce-sodden wedges took precedence over a recital of my day's activities. Conversation degenerated into questions and answers— the usual stuff: Where'd you go to school? How many brothers and sisters? Favorite music? Best movie? Best book?

Craig had graduated from Providence Vocational Technical Institute with an auto mechanic's certificate. He had two brothers, Steve and Bob, and a stepsister, Sarah. His father and stepmother still lived in Providence, the kids had "scattered."

He liked the Stones, Motley Crue, Springsteen— "Old stuff, mostly," he said around bites of pizza. "This new crap— it ain't rock 'n roll."

His favorite movie was "Terminator"—he'd seen it six times. As for books—

"I don't read much," he confessed with a smile. "Last book I read all the way through was the spec manual for my brother's Dodge."

In turn, I produced details about Parkville Senior High School and my handful of college credits; confessed the White Sheep as my sibling, named her husband and surprised myself by recalling the names of my nieces.

Craig shook his head. "My sister's always asking me when I'm going to settle down and get married," he said morosely. "She did it, see?— so it's got to be the way to go."

I laughed. "I remember Carol's face when I told her I'd left my husband. I've *never* seen a woman more relieved!"

He perked up a little. "You were married? What happened?"

"I was married— at nineteen. And what happened was we turned twenty." I shrugged. "He was a bass player, I was a secretary. We could have made it work, I guess, but neither one of us was really interested."

"Too bad. Were they any good?"

I blinked. "I'm sorry?"

"Your ex's band," Craig said patiently. "Were they any good?"

I thought back. "As a matter of fact, they were. They cut at least one record. After that— " I shrugged again, picked up a paper napkin and began to clean my hands. "I was out of the loop."

"Happens," Craig said and reached for the check lying face down by the grated cheese shaker. "Ready?"

The napkin was in shreds; my hands were as clean as they were going to get without soap and water. I dropped the shreds onto the soggy paper plate and got up, slinging my pocketbook over my shoulder.

"Ready."

He left a buck on the table for the waitress and paid the cashier with a crackling new twenty, accepted and pocketed his change. He held the door open for me to walk out into the cool, purple evening and stood too close to me on the sidewalk, his hand just touching my elbow.

I moved a step away, bringing the pocketbook around between us as I rooted for the car keys. Beneath my feet, the sidewalk shuddered and I heard the familiar squeak-and-grumble as the bulky old car turned onto Main Street from Preble.

"What the hell is that?" Craig demanded and I looked up from my search to see him staring in disbelief at the bottle-green hugeness of it, rumbling down the center of Main Street.

I laughed and summoned up my best Maine accent. "Not from aroun' heah, are you, young fella?" The behemoth screamed and came to a hissing stop across from us as I pointed. "That there's the Division. Goes right over the river into Waterville. Maybe you'd like to take a ride."

Craig seemed to shake himself before looking down at me. He was smiling, sort of, his eyes brilliantly blue.

"Maybe I would," he said. "Let's go."

# 14

CRAIG PAID THE FARE— two dollar bills deposited in the tall glass rectangle at the colonel's right hand— and stayed where he was, staring down into the cockpit.

Given Colonel Lyons' style, such a position was no less than suicidal. I slipped into the long bench on the left and grabbed the shiny brass guardrail.

Not a moment too soon. Colonel Lyons worked the lever, the doors came to with a clash, steel wheels screamed against steel track and the Division lurched forward.

Craig staggered, made a one-handed grab for the catch-pole, snagged it and then leaned, swaying at the length of his arm, over Colonel Lyons' shoulder.

"Nice-looking train," he yelled over the roar and rumble of the Division's progress. "What's she go on?"

"'lectric," the colonel yelled back. He spared Craig a half-glance over his shoulder. "She ain't a train, neither. This here's a trolley. Waterville and Wimsy Railroad, Electric Track Division. Established 1926. Oldest continuously-run 'lectric track on the Eastern Seaboard." He slammed the throttle down.

The Division shrieked to a halt. Craig swayed sharply, his fingers slid on the catch-pole— clamped hard. The colonel worked the lever and the doors crashed open.

"Best find yourself a seat," he told Craig, nodding toward the windshield. "Windscreen there's original— hate to see a crack in it."

"Yeah... thanks." Craig did an in-place about-face, slid past the woman mounting the steps toward the fare-box and came to rest beside me on the stiff leather bench.

"Hey, this is a hoot," he confided, as the doors closed and the Division lunged forward. "It just run on special days or what?"

"It runs Monday through Saturday, from seven a.m. to nine p.m.— the track's all over Wimsy. Used to be all over Waterville, too. In its heyday there were six cars, a line into Winslow and a spur down to Vassalboro."

"Sounds great." Craig looked around him with a grin. "So now it's down to one? I guess that makes sense, with everybody having a car— not much use for a trolley."

"Actually," I said, "the Division makes enough money to keep Colonel Lyons going— he's the sole owner, now. When the passenger trains pulled out of Maine, he took the Division— this car here— and a paper giving him track-right instead of his retirement money."

Craig laughed. "Crazy."

I frowned, thinking about money, and about the Division, which performed a real service for those who had no car, or a car unexpectedly in the shop, or who simply preferred to let someone else drive them across the river, and about Colonel Lyons, whose passion and driving force the Division was.

"Maybe," I said, but Craig was gawking at the varnished oak ceiling and I don't think he heard.

The Division howled to a halt, doors flying open. An elderly man laboriously made the climb from street to Division, favoring his left leg and leaning heavily on the rail. He didn't bother with the fare-box, just nodded at Colonel Lyons. "Norbert."

"Sam."

The doors closed, almost gently. The Division did not lurch immediately into action, but stood, tame and seemly, while Sam got situated in the jump-seat behind the driver's bay.

"That's all right," he said, and the Division leapt forward.

"See where ol' Righteous won't be playing the ponies much as he used to," Sam shouted over the din.

"That's a shame," Colonel Lyons returned. "Real loss to the local economy."

Sam laughed. The Division swung suddenly left, flinging me hard into Craig's shoulder, and conversation was impossible as we clamored, clattered and yowled our way across the Wimsy bridge.

\*\*\*

WE ALL DISEMBARKED at the Loop— the last piece of Division track in Waterville, in existence only because the lot belonged to prominent Waterville attorney and train buff William F. Abbott. He supplied the land, Colonel Lyons supplied the track, and the Waterville and Wimsy Railroad Electric Track Division, in these diminished days, was intact.

There was a group of eight or nine waiting patiently in the dusk— lunch boxes and grocery bags; an old lady holding a little girl's hand. The little girl had a plush dinosaur cradled precariously against her chest.

I paused at the edge of the Loop, Craig at my side. "Now where?" he asked.

"Want to see the sights of the city?" I returned. "Or catch the Division back to Wimsy?"

"It runs 'til nine, right?"

I nodded.

He checked his watch— an expensive looking Rolex. "We've got a couple hours. Why not take in the town?"

"You betcha." I pointed downhill. The lights were just coming on in the Concourse. "There she is— all of Waterville lies panting at your feet."

"Cool." Craig threw me a grin and stepped onto the sidewalk, keeping to the far edge to protect the lady from traffic, just like his mom'd taught him. I shifted my pocketbook to the right shoulder and went with him, walking down the long, slow hill to Waterville.

***

WE CAME IN THROUGH THE Concourse; windowshopped the Hallmark store, gazed at the displays of candied fruit and salted nuts in the Villager's window, gave up a tour of Ames and the Shop 'n Save in favor of cutting through the parking lot to the shops on the other side. There was a new bookstore in the Arcade Beneath— I made a mental note to visit real soon. Next door, The Blue Macaw was just closing— Craig blinked as a jungle bird's cry reverberated from within.

"They really do have a macaw— well, a green parrot— in there," I told him and he shook his head.

"Crazy."

Windowshopping and making minor conversation, we came to the top of the Concourse and turned down Silver Street, to Main.

At the corner, we stared into the Paragon Shop's overstuffed window, blinking at the crowd of pottery, colored glass, and tapestries, then crossed Main and started uptown.

"What's the crowd?" asked Craig, pointing up-walk, across Common Street.

"Must be a do at Sterns," I said, tucking my hands into jacket pockets. It was cool under Waterville's vapor lights, with the sun finally gone and the cars rushing by.

"Sterns?" Craig's eyebrows were high. "Like the department store?"

"Actually, yes. The building used to be a Sterns Department Store. They closed a couple of years ago and it was empty for a while. Then some movers and shakers decided that what Waterville needed was a center for the arts— so now it's the Sterns Cultural Center. There's some shops, an art gallery, and a theater— music, plays, dance recitals, that kind of stuff."

"Pretty fancy," Craig decided as we came to the edge of the crowd.

It must be children's night, I thought, considering the crowd blocking the walk. There was a smattering of adults, but most were kids, between nine, say, and thirteen. They were standing in a ragged column one to four children wide, which may have been an attempt at a line. I hesitated, trying to decide if it would be more efficient to go around or through—

"Jen!"

A chair moved in the crowd, jockeying for space; kids made room for it, and it shot free, skidding to a halt about an inch from my toes.

"Marian! Hey, what's going on?"

She made a face. "School trip. *Beauty and The Beast.* In ballet."

A local production, then. I grinned. "It might not be so bad." Belatedly, I introduced my walking companion. "Marian, this is Craig."

Craig what? I wondered suddenly, but no such difficulties assailed Marian. She barely glanced at him— "Hi"— before she was back on me.

"Jen, guess what? Fox had that weird screwdriver and

he brought it over for me to use and he's nice. He didn't try to poke his fingers in or make me do it his way and he said I can borrow his stuff, if there's something I don't have, just let him know—"

I stared, fighting disbelief. This animated person chattering before me was *not* Marian. Marian was adult-aloof, even closemouthed, nearer to computer than girl.

Whatever else Fox was— *nice?*— he was clearly a magician of some note.

"That's great," I told her, since she seemed to have run out of steam temporarily. "So you fixed the glitch?"

"Oh, that!" Marian dismissed the glitch with a flick of pale fingers. "That was the easy part. After I got the— "

"Marian!" The word was uttered in tones of gentle reproach. The woman who spoke was five or six years younger than me: short, pillow-soft and brightly blonde. She gave me a disapproving look out of pale blue eyes and glanced at Craig from beneath her lashes. Her hands were plump, soft and ringless.

"Marian, you know that you were to be in line with the others. We're almost ready to take you in now."

Marian visibly clenched, the animation draining out of her face. In the pink glow of the vapor lights she looked abruptly old and ill.

"I'm sorry, Ms. Heath," she said colorlessly. She looked up at me. "See you later, Jen."

"Call me," I told her. "Let me know how it is."

Her eyes flicked to Craig. "Sure."

She spun the chair and went back to the crowd of her classmates. Ms. Heath gave me one more sorrowful look and followed.

A moment later, Craig and I detoured around the mob scene, going into Main Street to do it.

We walked a little in silence, past Al Corey's music

store. The snow-white baby grand glittered in its spotlight behind the plate glass window.

"So," Craig said, glancing down at me from lash-shielded blue eyes, "you into computers?"

It was meant to be casual, but the tone was somewhere between disbelief and trepidation. I stifled a laugh.

"Some— not as much as Marian is. I built the machine I use at home— " I hesitated on the edge of sharing details of motherboard, RAM and BIOS, bit my tongue and settled for:

"I use it for writing and balancing the checkbook, mostly." And for running the boards— but Craig would never in a hundred years comprehend the lure of computer bulletin boards.

"Friend of mine has a real hotshot computer," he offered. "Speakers and a color screen. Showed me some of his games and the— "

I glanced away, up Main Street: a brown Chevette jumped out of Temple Street against the light and dove across two lanes of traffic, directly into the path of an elderly Lincoln.

Horror hit, and I yelled, wanting to close my eyes, to cover my ears, to be light-years and planets away. Impact was forgone, the Chevette would be crushed between the Lincoln and the opposite row of parked cars. There would be blood and broken glass and—

The Lincoln swerved, brakes squealing, into the parallel lane, cutting off a Nissan. The driver of the smaller car braked hard, and the Lincoln was miraculously in the clear. The Chevette completed its turn and took off, too fast, toward Winslow.

I sagged, relieved and vaguely ashamed.

"You okay?" Craig asked, reasonably enough.

"Yeah." I sighed, lifted a hand to comb the hair off my

forehead. "Yeah. Sorry about that."

"What's the deal?"

I hesitated, loath to drag it all out one more time, furious at myself for having done it *again*. It had been *years*— I shook myself and sighed again.

"Car crashes run in my family," I told Craig briefly. "I was in a bad one about five years ago— guy ran a red light and hit me broadside. My father'd always complained about my driving— too fast, he said, and I was going to wind up getting pried out of a wreck someday." I shrugged; my left shoulder, damaged by the flight through the windshield five years ago, was starting to ache.

"Anyhow, even though the accident wasn't my fault, it was like prophecy come true for my dad." I bit my lip, and closed it fast. "He barely finished saying 'I told you so' before he wrapped himself and my mom around a telephone pole."

"Hey, that's tough," Craig said, with a notable lack of sympathy. "No wonder you were shook up." He turned and resumed his interrupted stroll toward Temple Street.

After a minute, I followed him.

\*\*\*

WE CAUGHT THE NINE o'clock Division and in due time alighted before the Wimsy House of Pizza. Jerry, the owner, was turning the Open sign around to Closed. He waved, then turned a speculative eye on Craig.

*Great,* I thought grumpily. *By tomorrow morning I'll be engaged and by tomorrow night I'll be married.*

This was simply the small-town way, but tonight it peeved me mightily, and I stayed peeved during the short drive from downtown to the house on the point. Which I guess is why I was a bit more abrupt than I might otherwise have been when Craig walked me to my door and leaned over for a kiss.

I'm not a cruel person. There's nothing to be gained by lacerating the feelings of someone you have no intention in the world of kissing. I stepped back, smiling and shaking my head, which is usually enough.

Not for Craig. Craig was a man inclined to kiss the nearest acceptable object; a man whose passion would brook no missish nay-saying. He leaned in again, eyes at half-mast in the porch light's glow, lips slightly parted.

I went back a step, peevishness going up a notch toward annoyance.

"Forget it."

Shock hit; blue eyes went wide and he straightened, staring down at me with— with *nothing* in his face. I shivered. Annoyance took a detour through alarm.

"Hey," he said softly, and there wasn't much in the voice either. "That's not nice."

I took a deep breath and met those expressionless eyes with the best glare I could muster.

"I'm not the kissing type," I told him. "Nothing personal, Craig." I stuck my right hand out. "Goodnight."

For a second I thought he was going to insist. I had enough time to think about my nearest neighbor, half-a-mile away through the woods.

Craig brought his hand up. Shook. There seemed to be something in his face now, but I could not have said what.

"Okay," he said. "Goodnight."

I watched him leave the porch, get in Morris' truck and start the engine. He backed carefully around and drove sedately up the drive.

When I could no longer hear the truck's engine, I went across to the Camaro, parked under the old oak. My hands were shaking— ice cold. I fumbled the key into the ignition and drove into the barn. Then I went up the ell into the house and, for the second time in four days, locked the kitchen door.

\*\*\*

I WOKE UP WITH THE third nightmare around two— confused images of twisted, burning metal, Butchie Stern's body lying tidy and lifeless, Marian's eyes dying as I watched, and Craig, his face full of nothing...

"Damn." I swung out of bed in the dark, pulled on my robe and padded barefoot down the hall, tying the sash as I went.

The computer came alive at the touch of a switch, screen bathing the room in ghost-light. I called up the dial-list, intending to call the Net and check my mail. At the moment of choosing, my unsteady hand twitched, the pointer touched another number and clicked.

Inside the computer, seven almost-musical notes sounded, followed by a connect.

*Welcome,* the screen announced: *You have reached Random Access BBS ....*

Well, why not?

At the prompt, I typed in my name and password and was admitted without hesitation to the board.

\*\*\*

MY SECURITY LEVEL had been increased, allowing access to several other message bases and an astonishing library of files available for download. The night-worries receded as I explored those— *Fox must have a CD hooked into the board*, I thought and then changed my mind.

*He must have TWO CDs in tandem....*

Eventually, I emerged from the library, metaphorically dusty and much calmer. I paused at the main menu to survey my options.

*Page the Sysop* caught my eye. I'd heard a BBS page from the sysop side— once. It was a sound combining the worst parts of ambulance, fire engine and cop-car sirens. After that, I always thought twice before paging any sysop.

I thought three times now. It would be nice, I thought, to chat with Fox. On the other hand it was closing in on three a.m. and nothing short of a discovered virus or hacker invasion was justification for—

The screen blanked; reformed in an eyeblink, bisected by a thin white line.

*Hello, Jennifer, Fox here.*

Relief— idiotic, illogical relief— washed through me.

*You're up late,* I commented.

*I might say the same to you.*

*And just did.*

I hesitated; typed: *Couldn't sleep.* And then:

*The cops arrested Scott Ash. Murder.*

*Oh, no.* Fox's response was instantaneous. *How's his wife?*

*Scared. Pissed. Says he didn't do it. Nautrally.* I hesitated, but my fingers kept on. *Says she knows who did.*

*Yes? That could prove useful. Did she tell the cops?*

*There's a problem.* I took a deep gulp of air, watching the words leap into being on the screen.

*She knows— she says she knows— because Scott had a vision.*

There was a slight pause, before:

*You don't believe in visions?*

*Do you?* My fingers challenged before I could stop them.

*No,* Fox typed slowly. *I believe in ghosts.* There was a longer pause, then, still typing slow: *I understand the difficulty in bringing this intelligence to the attention of the police. What will you do?*

I blinked in surprise. *Me? It doesn't have anything to do with me.*

Which was, I thought suddenly, a flat lie. In spite of my cogitations yesterday afternoon, it had everything to do with me. I'd seen Scott leaving the scene of the crime.

I was— very likely— Bruce Gagnon's prize witness.

*Oh, hell,* my fingers were telling Fox, *I only just realized. Bruce is going to use me— my testimony — to hang Scott.*

*Maine doesn't have the death penalty.* Fox reminded me.

*No, but they do have life imprisonment.* I shivered and closed my eyes. Locked up for the rest of your days, when all you'd wanted was to get the sheep under roof... I swallowed, hard. Opened my eyes and looked at the clock in the corner of the screen. Three twenty-six.

*I should let you get some sleep,* I told Fox, and blatantly changed the subject.

*Thanks for helping Marian out by the way— she tells me you're nice, which is a signal honor. Marian never thinks anyone is nice.*

*On the contrary,* Fox typed. *She told me that you were nice.* A very slight pause.

*Good night, Jennifer. I hope you'll be able to sleep now.*

*I hope so, too,* I returned. *CYA.*

*CYA.*

A flicker of color and I was back in the board.

Reluctantly, I chose <G> for goodbye from the main menu and left Random Access behind.

# 15

THE ALARM CLOCK LET loose and I rolled over, grabbed it and pushed in the pin. The racket cut off in mid-clang. I collapsed back onto the pillow, clock cradled in my hands, and took stock.

My head was pounding, which was expectable, given the dreams and the night and the worries. Likewise expectable was the hot-wire crankiness in my bad shoulder and the all-over gritty feeling. Sleep would take care of the headache and the grittiness, at least. I closed my eyes and tried to remember my schedule.

This was Tuesday: meeting day. On Tuesday I usually went in at three, covered the selectmen's meeting or the comprehensive plan meeting or the school board meeting at seven, back at eight, eight-thirty, to write the story....

Not this Tuesday.

Abruptly, it came clear. *This* Tuesday I was day-news, covering Milt Vane's shift. *This* Tuesday I had to be in Town Hall at ten o'clock sharp for a meeting with a suit from the Maine Harness Racing Commission. Milt had turned this one down cold, which was predictable. Since the suit was unlikely to be female— there was by definition nothing in the story for Milt to sink his teeth into— and so he told Bill Jacques.

Rather than enter into a protracted hassle, Bill rewrote the schedule, giving me the racing commissioner and Milt the school board. Even Milt had sense enough not to squawk about that.

Ten o'clock at Town Hall, alert and intelligent.

Shit. I opened my eyes and lifted the clock.
Eight-fifteen.
Groaning, I went to take a shower.

***

TWENTY MINUTES LATER, dressed in black corduroy slacks and a red cotton turtleneck, I hit the kitchen. Water and grounds went into the coffee maker; I flicked the switch to "on" and stood mindlessly watching the drip until something flashed by my shoulder, hitting the window over the sink with a loud *thump*.

I started, swinging around fast, hand raised to fend off God-knew-what.

From his perch on the sill, Jasper blinked lazy hazel eyes and turned his attention to the world outside the pane.

"Terrify me, why don't you?" I snapped, absurdly embarrassed. Nervously, I touched the silver studs in my ears before crossing to the fridge.

I've never been a big eater and breakfast has never been my favorite meal. During most of my adult life I've gotten along with a cup of coffee and a slice of toast for the repast my mother had taught me was "the essential meal of the day." This morning, even toast looked like a lot of trouble.

Gritting my teeth, I hauled out the bread and slid a slice gently into the depths of my aunt's elderly two-slicer. While breakfast was burning, I poured out the absolutely essential coffee, added milk and carried the mug to the table, returning a moment later with my buttered slice. Sliding into a chair, I proceeded to eat, grimly deliberate, and trying unsuccessfully to ignore the pounding of my head.

It was going to be a bad day. I *hated* this— hated the heaviness behind my eyes and the way the sluggish thoughts seemed to burn the surface of my brain. I hated it even more than I hated the tired, familiar ache in the damaged shoulder. And it was only tension. I *knew* that. I put my elbows on the table and rubbed my eyes.

"Damn."

In Baltimore, I had headaches often. In Baltimore, I'd had a prescription— magic blue pills to keep the headaches at bay.

In Maine, where I'd lived nearly two years without the whisper of a migraine, I'd let the prescription expire.

The toast sat uneasy on my stomach. I took my hands away from my eyes and considered the pale brown liquid steaming gently in the ceramic mug.

"Prrt?"

It was an odd noise, perfectly unlike any other noise I'd ever heard, but with a definite note of inquiry attached. It had come from the direction of the floor. I looked down.

Jasper was sitting by my chair, ears alert, eyes alight with interest.

"Prrt?" he inquired again.

And leapt into my lap.

Unprecedented. Jasper had never shown the least desire for my company, going so far as to look pointedly away from an offered introductory finger. Now, I sat frozen as he purred and kneaded, then curled 'round against my stomach, still rumbling and looking almost unbearably pleased with himself.

Tentatively, I extended a finger. Jasper politely touched it with his nose. I stroked his head and his rumbling increased.

This was astonishing. Carefully, I picked up the coffee mug and sipped; Jasper squinted his eyes in pleasure. I put my free hand around the curve of his back. I was not dissuaded by so much as an ear-flick.

"You're not sick, are you, cat?"

No answer. Well, I hadn't really expected one.

I drank coffee, taking my time about it, then sat, eyes closed, for a time, both hands tucked around Jasper, feeling his purrs vibrate against my palms. I may have dozed off for a minute or five. When I opened my eyes, the readout on the microwave stood at nine-thirty-five. I sighed, and, very gently, stirred.

"Time for me to go," I told Jasper, and then, feeling slightly foolish, "Thanks."

I shifted once more, trying not to rush it. Jasper jumped to the floor, stretched and walked away, tail high. I got up, brushed white fur off my black slacks, plucked pocketbook and jacket from the peg by the door and went down the ell to the barn.

\*\*\*

COLIN WYANDOTTE OF the Maine Harness Racing Commission was short, thin and affable. Though he was, in fact, wearing a suit, he didn't look particularly comfortable in it. He'd loosened his tie by the time I shook hands with him, and opened the first button on his white broadcloth shirt.

"From The *Voice*, eh? Fine paper. Bill Jacques still writing for you?"

I smiled and told him that Bill was news editor, nowadays, and his face lit with what looked like genuine pleasure.

"Well, now, that's fine. Good to see an able man rewarded. Used to see Bill when I was driving— fair circuit, understand. Saw him a little less when I come to be an owner, though he did call me once or twice for something on one of his stories. Able man. You tell him I said so." He grinned and shook his head. "What we come to, eh? Driving a desk, that's what it all boils down to, in the end."

He seemed to shake himself, then, and waved toward the battered conference table. "Mustn't keep you all morning," he said, "Let's sit down and you can ask me your questions."

We sat. I flipped open my notebook, uncapped the Bic and gave Mr. Wyandotte a smile that sent tiny sparks of pain through my aching head.

"What makes the racing commission think an off-track betting parlor would be good for Wimsy?" A loaded question, in its way. Let's see what he would make of it.

He caught it without a blink, tucked it under his arm and ran with it.

Over the next twenty minutes I was treated to a history of track betting in the state of Maine, and a concise comparison of those trends with betting trends in other New England states.

"The tracks had a certain unsavory reputation attached to them— I'm not going to try to hide that from you." Colin Wyandotte grinned. "Bill Jacques would only put you straight on it when you got back anyway, so why waste my time?" The grin faded. "As that reputation took hold, people shied away from visiting the tracks, bets fell off, legitimate trainers, legitimate owners—, Maine people— were robbed of a significant source of income. The Commission and the Off-Track Betting Committee are trying to take that back. Betting parlors will be sited in up-scale restaurants, like the Mill, here in Wimsy. There will be big-screen TVs for viewing the races; bets will be placed by computer— they look something like a lottery machine, understand. The technology is very solid.

"The set-up will discourage abuse, will keep the undesirable elements out, and make it possible for Maine people to make money and to enjoy the pleasures of high-stakes racing."

Not bad for an ex-driver. I glanced up from my notes. "What undesirable elements?"

Mr. Wyandotte blew air and leaned back in his chair, eyes traveling toward the ceiling.

"Well, now." He looked back to me. "Not from around here, I take it? Not with that accent."

"Midcoast," I confessed calmly. "Maryland."

"Maryland," he repeated, like he'd actually heard of the state. "Some fine racing done in Maryland." He cocked his head.

"City girl?" he asked. "Or out of chicken country?"

"Baltimore."

"Well, then." He looked at me, head cocked. "I expect this won't shock you like it might some others." He straightened in his chair.

"See, Maine's a small state, population-wise. We're not all piled up on top one another like down Baltimore, or even like some other New England states. Rhode Island, Connecticut— it's a shame how they've crowded themselves up 'til they got no room to breathe. It's not like that up here— oh, we got the Canadian border, and there's probably some money to be made down Portland, Kittery-way. But there's not much up here to attract the Mafia. And we intend to keep it that way. The betting stations are computerized; the attendants will be state employees. There'll be no monkeying with the odds or any other cunning trick like they might play down Rhode Island. No sir." He smiled faintly.

"We make it tough enough and they'll stay home. The bottom line just isn't there."

The Mafia. Despite Mr. Wyandotte's assumption, I *was* shocked. The Mafia belonged to cities, to drugs, to sudden bodies bleeding out their lives in back alleys. The Mafia stood behind Baltimore's Block— at least, most people thought so. The Mafia owned New York City, lock, stock and skyscraper.

But Wimsy? In Wimsy everybody knew everybody else. A stranger would stick out like a red barn in a snowstorm.

"Anything else I can answer for you?"

Mr. Wyandotte's voice pulled me back to now. I glanced down, flipped rapidly through my notes and glanced up with what I hoped was a smile.

"You've done beautifully," I told him. "I've got everything I need."

"Well, now, that's fine." He stood, reached into his inside jacket pocket and pulled out a leatherette case from which he extracted, with some difficulty, a business card.

"Call me if you need something more," he said, holding the card out. "Always glad to help the press."

"Thank you." I took the card and slid it into my pocketbook with the rest of my equipment, stood and shook his hand. "You've been very helpful."

"My pleasure. Remember to tell Bill I asked after him."

"I'll do that," I promised and escaped into the searing brightness of a late October morning.

# 16

SUNLIGHT ASSAULTED ME; lancing from the sky, stabbing off of shop windows. I bent my head, but sunlight found me still, reflecting into my face from the concrete walk.

My stomach churned and it was hard to say which was more blinding, the pain in my head or the pitiless onslaught of light.

I had to get out of the sun. The Camaro was parked in the municipal lot by the river, two blocks away. It might as well have been two miles. Cautiously, I raised my head, surveying my surroundings through slitted eyes.

Directly before me was Kelly's Kraft Korner, window awash in corn husks. Just 'round the corner from Kelly's was Mother's Pantry, Gaia Coven's co-op. There were chairs in Mother's. Chairs and a couple of tiny round tables, where you could sit and sip a cup of herbal tea and nibble a "natural" goodie. Most important, it was out of the sun.

Slowly, head bowed once more and eyes squinted almost closed, I got myself around the corner and into Mother's Pantry.

The bell over the door rattled when I came in, rattled again as I pushed the door to. The shop was empty. I made it to the first table and sat down heavily, back to the door.

It was dim, blessedly dim. I closed my eyes and concentrated on breathing— even, if not particularly deep, breaths. The air was cool, tasting of spice and mint. After a time— I'm not sure how long— I was able to open my eyes.

"Better now?" asked the woman opposite me. She blinked solemnly behind owl-round glasses and added, "You don't look too good, if you don't mind my saying so."

"As it happens, I don't feel too good," I told her; the words came out kind of cottony and thick.

"We have a match," she intoned and grinned. The grin faded and she tipped her head, studying me. "Mind if I ask— no, it's a migraine, isn't it? I can see it in your eyes." She pushed her chair back and rose. "I'll make you some tea."

The last thing I wanted was something else arguing with my stomach. "Tea? I don't— "

"Tea," she interrupted firmly, pushing a wisp of blonde hair behind her right ear. She looked at me, glasses glinting, obscuring her expression. "Nice tea. Peppermint. Rosemary. Chamomile. A little honey. You'll like it." She turned and marched off, sandals silent on the wooden floor.

I closed my eyes and breathed for awhile, savoring the flavor of the air. Music wafted, borne on the flavorful air— harps, bells, drums.

"Okay, just sip this— no hurry, but it's better if you drink it warm."

There was a soft clink of china settling onto wood. I opened my eyes. Before me sat a white china teacup on a fluted base, painted all over with red roses. Inside the cup a faintly green liquid steamed gently. I did indeed smell mint, and a sweet edge of honey, as well as other unidentifiable green flavors. I glanced over at my hostess, who had resumed her seat across from me.

"Thanks."

"No problem. Boy, I hate a migraine. I used to get them all the time."

"I did, too." I picked up the dainty cup on the fingertips of both hands, sipped cautiously. Mint and honey were the overwhelming sensations. I suspected they were there to mask less pleasant herbal tastes.

"I haven't had a migraine since I've been in Maine," I said, lowering the cup. "Got cocky and let my medicine run out."

"Nothing wrong with that— those drugs are bad for you." She grinned and the glasses glinted. "I know, I sound like a Granola. Happens I am a Granola."

"Another match," I murmured, and she outright laughed.

"From the wash-and-wear hair right down to the ergonomically correct sandals. If the girls at Vassar could see me now."

I looked at her over the rim of the teacup. She was about my age, I thought— full-faced, with fine blond hair parted in the middle and cut off blunt at the line of her jaw. The eyes behind the owl-glasses were gray. She looked familiar, but then everybody in Wimsy looks familiar to me now.

"You're Jennifer Pierce, aren't you?" she asked.

Another one. There is no privacy in a small town. "Right."

"Thought so. I'm Elizabeth Paul."

No wonder she looked familiar. "The midwife."

"Good memory," she said. "Drink your tea."

I complied while my brain sluggishly marshaled information. Eliza Paul, as the popular vernacular had it, was a registered nurse, licensed midwife, and self-styled herb lady.

She was also chairperson of Central Maine Choice, an organization which had set its face firmly against everything Hyannis Stern preached. And she had graduated Vassar, Class of '79.

I set the empty cup down.

"Guess things'll be slow for you, now Reverend Stern's dead."

She snorted. "I wish. Unfortunately, there's no shortage of assholes to take over his slot. Though even the worst of those knows to keep his hands in his pockets."

I must have looked as stupid as I felt. What was this? Butchie as lady-killer? But why not, after all? He'd been an attractive enough man, in a suit-and-silk-tie kind of way.

"I guess it was before your time," Eliza Paul said, with the tip of the head I was beginning to recognize as characteristic of her. "We were doing a counter-picket on ol' Righteous out at the Pittsfield Medical Center. Him and his ghouls lined up on one side of the door, CMC lined up on the other side. Things were tense, but under control. Then comes this couple up the walk. She's obviously having contractions. He's carrying the suitcase, hand on her elbow— young. Sixteen. Eighteen. Wedding rings on both of them. Going to the hospital to birth their baby, just like in the fairy tales." She shook her head, mouth thinning.

"Our group stepped back to give them room. You'd've thought Righteous would've gotten down on his knees and kissed their feet."

"Not?" I guessed.

"Worse. Just as they're coming up to the doors, one of the ghouls breaks rank, *lunges* at the girl, shoving this— *picture...*" She broke off, lenses glinting.

"I've seen them."

"Right. So the kid lets out a yell and her husband shoves the ghoul and grabs her, and one of *my* group jumps out of line, gets in front of the ghoul, blocks his sign with hers. The doors open, a couple orderlies come flying out, surround the kids and bring them through. In the meantime, the ghoul's screaming like the damned, and my girl's giving back as good as she gets. I move out to get her, to break it up, but Righteous is already there and he's in my girl's face, screaming at her and she's giving it back to him, and he's getting all red in the face, and suddenly she's down on her ass on the sidewalk with the ghoul and Righteous towering over her...."

I sat up. "He *pushed* her?"

Eliza nodded. "That's what she said. But the ghoul and Righteous said she fell, and the cop didn't think it was worth the hassle to get the truth. Righteous got a warning. We all got a lecture."

"Terrific."

She shrugged. "Hey, why haul us in and make life inconvenient for himself? Why do all that work, just to let us go home, when if he didn't do *any* work, we'd go home even sooner?"

"Point," I allowed, and sighed. The headache seemed to have ebbed; my stomach, while still queasy, was no longer giving me cause for immediate concern. "So what happened?"

"Nothing."

"Nothing?"

"Well, nothing ever did happen to Righteous, did it? That mail campaign he was doing— you were here for that, weren't you?"

The mail campaign was before my time, too, but I'd heard all about it from Dan Skat, whose eight-year-old daughter had been first to the mailbox the day Butchie's full-color mangled fetus postcard arrived. I nodded, cautiously.

Eliza waved a hand. "Terrorizing through the mails is what it was. I went to the postmaster myself. The postmaster spoke to the Reverend. The Reverend obliged the postmaster by sending his little horrors out in envelopes. The postmaster is happy and doesn't really understand why I'm not." She sighed gustily. "Maine."

I grinned, which was almost bearable. "I have a friend

who says she'll move to Maine if there's ever a nuclear war because it takes everything twenty years to get here."

Eliza laughed. "Too true. So, anyhow, nothing happened to Righteous, as per usual, and Righteous continued on his merry way. From then on we made sure we put the biggest and the toughest on our front line. If it ever came down to shoving again, I knew who I wanted to see kissing concrete."

"Nice man," I murmured. "Made a lot of friends."

"Wherever he went," Eliza said. "Unfortunately."

"Yeah," I agreed, "but he didn't hang out in the *best* places." She chuckled and I put a finger on the rim of the teacup. "How much do I owe you?"

"First one's free," she said comfortably. "I can mix you up some leaf to take home, if you want. Cost you couple bucks."

I hesitated. The headache was not by any means gone. But I felt like a functioning unit, which I definitely hadn't when I'd come in.

"Sure," I told Eliza. "Can't hurt."

"That's the spirit. Just take a second."

She was out of her chair and across the room, light and confident. I closed my eyes and listened to the wafting, wind-chimey music until I heard paper crackling nearby and opened my eyes.

"There you go." Eliza put the bag on the table; the opening was neatly folded into a flap and stapled. Pierced with the brown paper was a white card bearing tiny, meticulous writing.

"I wrote down the ingredients and how much to use at one time. No more than four cups a day, okay?""

"Okay," I agreed and reached into my pocketbook for cash.

\*\*\*

I WAS JUST ON TIME for my second stop of the day— the ninety-seventh birthday of Mrs. Alice Boudreau, resident of River's Edge Retirement Home in East Wimsy.

The big common room was draped in pink streamers, there were pink balloons by the hundreds, staff and resident-guests wore pink party hats.

Dan Skat was already there, taking a picture of the guest of honor.

"Where's your pink hat?" I whispered to him as he clipped the cap over his lens.

"Where's yours?"

"Pink isn't my color."

He grinned. "Doesn't seem to be many people's color, but it's not stopping them," he observed and turned away. "See ya. Have a nice interview."

As it happened, the interview went like a dream. Mrs. Boudreau was sharp as a tack, witty and gracious. I got some first class stuff from her, some nice bits from the nursing supervisor and staff head about how they were lucky to have her with them, and slipped away before they cut the cake.

It wasn't until I was in the Camaro, radio up, windows down and on the way back to the *Voice*, that I realized my headache was gone.

\*\*\*

I WAS PROOFREADING THE Boudreau story when a shadow crossed the keyboard. The half-wall behind Karen's Computer creaked as someone leaned on it. Warily, more than half-expecting Milt Vane, I glanced up.

Bill Jacques nodded. "Afternoon, Miz Pierce."

"Good afternoon, Mr. Jacques," I returned, folding my hands primly on my lap. "What can I do for you today?"

"It's tomorrow that you can do something for me," he said. "I've taken the liberty of changing your schedule, since I know you'll want to see your story through to the grand finale."

Old-news courtesy, that. In this day of unions and mandated shift-change, a reporter rarely had the opportunity to follow her story from start to end. You learned not to care, Carly the copy editor told me, when a rushed or careless colleague garbled facts or names you had cold.

I smiled into Bill Jacques' blunt face. "Thanks," I said and meant it. "What's doing?"

"The Medical Examiner has released Reverend Stern's mortal remains," he said, without a quiver of levity. "The funeral is tomorrow, two p.m., at Rand Funeral Home, followed by interment in Garden Cemetery. A mood piece. Dan'll swing by the cemetery for a shot of the assembled mourners." He raised his eyebrows. "Want it?"

"Want it," I affirmed.

"Good." He straightened.

"I'll have this one ready for you in another couple minutes," I said, nodding at the screen. "Anything else you need from me today?"

"Your shift's over, isn't it?" asked Bill. "Go on home and let Milt do some work. For a change." He went back to his desk.

I finished proofreading the Boudreau story, spell-checked, coded and sent it. Then I shut down Karen's Computer, tidied the desk and gathered up my stuff.

"Any questions on that?" I asked Bill on my way out.

"They both look clean," he said, eyes never leaving his screen. "You going to be home, if I have a question later?"

I raised my eyebrows. "Where else would I be?"

# 17

THERE'D BEEN A TIME in the not-too-distant
past when I owned an entire closet full of clothes suitable
for wearing to funerals.

As administrative assistant to the titular head of a
college, I had not only been expected to run the place, but
dress "professionally." Thus I amassed a wardrobe of dark,
conservatively-cut suits, pastel polyester blouses,
coordinated accessories, and low-heeled dress shoes. The
Compleat Girl Friday.

The funny thing is, I never realized how much I
hated that damn uniform until I came to Wimsy.

The closet I faced now held cotton shirts in a bright
array of colors and patterns, slacks, jeans, T-shirts, some
early-season turtlenecks, a sweatshirt or two, a couple of
vests. From my position in the doorway, I couldn't see so
much as a *dress*, though I was certain I owned one.

Didn't I?

Frowning, I peered closer into the narrow depths of
the closet. I clearly recalled hauling the suits and the pretty
blouses out of the closet, folding everything neatly and
filling bag after bag with the sluffed skin of my former life.

The one-inch heels had gone into their own bag—
six pairs of them: one black, two brown, two navy, one
burgundy.

I'd dumped the contents of the jewelry box into a
heap in the center of the bed and sorted through the chains
and gidgets, retaining the few pieces I actually liked and
filling another bag with the rest.

After that, I'd put all the bags into the Camaro and

driven to the Goodwill Thrift Store in downtown Waterville, where I left bags and contents in the astonished but no-doubt capable hands of a volunteer named Giselle.

Then I'd driven home, feeling about a century younger, climbed the stairs and stared into the empty closet.

Except that it hadn't been— entirely— empty. I hadn't quite been heady enough to cut all the ties. *After all,* I remembered reasoning, *what if I have to go to a funeral?*

I stepped into the closet, reached out and began shoving clothes along the steel rod. The hangers skritched and squeaked along the metal and I shuddered against the sound.

And there, at the very back of the closet, a little flat from their long sojourn in the dark, were the items I sought.

A navy blue suit coat, very plain, matching A-line skirt and a white polyester blouse with fake pearl buttons and baby lace edging the high Victorian collar.

With a certain feeling of awe, I extracted these artifacts, shook them and hung them in the doorway, then returned to root along the closet floor, through sneakers, boots and walking shoes, for a pair of plain black pumps.

They were somewhat dusty, but otherwise exactly as I recalled. I cleaned them with the sleeve of my robe, then shucked the robe and dressed.

Pantyhose feel weird.

\*\*\*

MOURNERS HAD SPILLED out of Rand's biggest parlor and into the hallway, where they either milled or clumped, according to their own inclination. The result was a shifty, noisy maze that stretched from wall to wall and a good ten feet down the hall.

I straightened my shoulders and lifted my head, conscious of the weight of my hair. The suit had looked subtly wrong when I stood before the bathroom mirror; it had taken me an entire minute to spot the culprit.

In Baltimore, the Compleat Girl Friday had worn her hair stylishly if stringently short. In Maine, Jen Pierce had just let the stuff grow, stopping by Mainely Manes when I thought about it so Philip could cut my bangs. The result was a shoulder length mass of wavy dark hair that was totally wrong against the suit's stark efficiency.

I'd twisted and pinned a hasty bun, applied mascara and make-up in about twice the time it used to take when I performed such rituals every morning, then ran for the door.

And now that I was here, in the halls of mourning, I saw that I needn't have gone to one-tenth the trouble. I did spot a couple suits— not necessarily black— and several elderly ladies wearing hats and gloves. Elsewhere, there were jeans— clean for the occasion— work boots, flannel shirts; sports jackets that didn't quite match the slacks they were paired with. Few— very few— ties.

A typical crowd, which might be found relatively unchanged at concert, movie, church, play— or funeral. I should have known.

Feeling a little foolish, I stepped into the hall.

A shorter woman would have had rough sailing through that shifting maze of bodies. I set my sights on the door opposite and went for it at only slightly less than my normal stride. The crowd rearranged itself and let me by.

I paused in the doorway of the parlor to count the house. Many of these must be family, I decided: lots of black; somber men in dark suits and severe ties; women in unadorned black dresses, taupe stockings and uncomfortable-looking shoes; a scattering of subdued children, in dark blues and grays, standing respectfully by while the grown-ups spoke among themselves in whispers, as if they were afraid of waking up the guest of honor.

"Good afternoon." The voice was cultured, unctuous. I turned and looked down into the bland, unsorrowful face of a professional.

"Mr. Rand, how are you?"

Puzzlement momentarily disturbed his blandness, but the putty-colored eyes were sharp. He found me out behind my city duds within a single beat of my heart.

"Ah, Ms. Pierce. How good of you to come. I'm certain the family will be appreciative. Won't you sign the guest book?"

I did, and then moved into the room. Folding chairs had been set out in twelve orderly rows, facing front, the coffin and the podium. Some of the chairs were occupied, but most people were clustered in the back, talking, soft and somber.

I skirted the talkers and went down the aisle between the chairs. There was a red-velvet kneeler conveniently placed by the side of the casket, but I was damned if I would kneel to Butchie Stern, quick or quit. I stood and looked down at him laid out on white satin, dressed nattily as ever, hands folded on his chest, holding a single hothouse daisy, wedding band burnished mirror-bright against the waxen flesh.

His face in death was cold, devoid of humanity: a waxworks parody of a man's face, competently crafted, but without fire.

Dead. Dead and done. I turned from the casket.

From the fourth row of chairs, right side, a woman was waving at me. I frowned, cataloging curly gray hair, stocky figure in a neat blue-and-white shirtwaist, blue plastic buttons adorning each earlobe—

"*Harry?*" Disbelieving, I obeyed her summons, sat in the chair beside her and stared.

"What on earth have you done to yourself?" I demanded.

"Could ask you the same," she commented. Her grin was unchanged, gap-toothed and wicked. "Nice of Butchie to give us a chance to dress up and strut our stuff."

"Such stuff as we may have or what desire to strut it." I shook my head. "I would never have known you."

"Good thing one of us got eyes," she said, settling back.

"That's for sure. Where's Morris?"

"Not coming." Harry's face clouded momentarily. "Morris stopped comin' to funerals couple years back. Said they were startin' to feel too personal."

"I can see that. What are we waiting for, by the way?"

"Eulogy." She eyed me. "Don't they have funerals down the city?"

"Funerals are only one in a long list of entertainment options available to the citizens of Baltimore," I told her loftily, "and not the best-attended."

"Huh. Well, you'll like Reverend LaBelle. Gives a hell of a sermon."

"Praise indeed," I murmured, as Mr. Rand walked to the front of the room and discreetly tapped his palms together.

"If those present would please find seats," he suggested blandly. "Family members here, if you would be so kind— " A soft-handed flourish indicated the first three rows, which were cordoned off with a length of crepe.

People began to mill and cough and fill the rows. An usher came down the center aisle, an elderly, black-clad lady leaning heavily on his arm. Mr. Rand moved forward to remove the black crepe. The usher seated the lady first row center, his posture conveying sorrow and respect.

More black-clad figures came down the aisle, began to fill the front chairs. People flowed into our row, edged past Harry and me, until we were solid, wall to aisle.

There was some rustling and shuffling. One of the women up front burst noisily into tears, and was cuddled by the woman beside her, sobs muffled against a broad, black shoulder.

Eventually, there was quiet.

When the quiet had endured an entire two minutes, one last figure came down the center aisle, paused for a moment to gaze into the coffin, and proceeded to the podium.

He looked down at the podium, moving papers, I think, giving the audience a chance to check him out: a middling-tall man in a black suit, soft of body and thin of hair. His hands were pudgy, supremely certain among his shuffles of paper; there was a plain gold band on the ring finger of his left hand.

The last paper shifted. He looked up from the podium, round face serious, dark eyes liquid.

"I'm Robert LaBelle," he said, and his voice was a surprise— deep and mellifluous. "A good number of you here today know who I am. For those who don't, I'll say that I'm the pastor of Hillside Evangelical Church. But that's not why I'm here." He shook his head, face inexpressibly sad.

"No sir. Today, I'm here to tell you about my friend— my good friend, Righteous Stern."

There was a stir in the audience. Reverend LaBelle cocked his head, face betraying gentle puzzlement.

"What's that? You say that Righteous was a name used by my friend's enemies, to belittle and dismay him— to cast his soul into confusion?" He spread his hands, smiling softly. "But what should a Christian fear of righteousness?"

There was another stir at that and a leaning forward of some of the folks in rows one through three.

"Hyannis Stern was one of the most righteous men I knew," Reverend LaBelle went on. "When God spoke to him, he listened. When the path was hard, he persevered. His faith was stalwart in the face of many adversities and private sorrows. He performed the work for which he'd been chosen with courage and did not disdain to pray for those who abused him."

There was more— a lot more— in similar vein: highlights of Butchie's abortionist-hunting career, gentle hints of heavy private sorrows that plagued the great man's life, his "true Christianity, in which he rightly abhorred the sin, but never failed of cherishing the sinner."

I snuck my pad out onto my knee and noted down the choicer bits. Harry'd been right, Robert LaBelle preached a hell of a sermon, and it would make terrific copy for Bill Jacques' mood piece.

On the very edge of having spoken too long, Reverend LaBelle fell silent. Around the room men and women were weeping openly; the Reverend among them. He bent his head and visibly took himself in hand. When he raised his face again, it was wet, but lit with a sort of quiet jubilation.

"*Awake to righteousness, and sin not!*" he commanded, arms spread wide to embrace us all. He lowered them slowly and looked out across the audience; brought his right hand up and lay it, palm-flat, against his breast.

"Let us pray."

\*\*\*

I FOLLOWED THE HEARSE to the boneyard, one car in a long, long line, Harry strapped into the passenger's seat.

"Which one was Mrs. Stern?" I asked, keeping an eye on the bumper of the Chrysler in front of me.

"Eh? At least four Mrs. Sterns there— sons' wives."

"I meant Butchie's wife— widow." The Chrysler braked; I did the same, sighing softly.

"Her? She wasn't there."

I glanced over. "Why not?"

Harry's mouth tightened. She broke my gaze and looked out the side window.

"Because she's living on the fourth floor," she said after awhile.

I blinked. "Fourth floor" was a euphemism for "Waterville Hospital Mental Health Ward," which facility happened to occupy the fourth floor of the six-story hospital building.

"Butchie's death that much of a shock to her?"

Harry laughed, low and strained. "Nope. She's been living between Keller's Home and the fourth floor for the past year or so. Before that, she'd live at home between bouts— traveled with Butchie, when he went preaching." Harry sighed.

"I went to tell her about him dying," she said slowly. "What she did— she laughed. Kind of— chilled my blood, you understand."

"I understand," I said softly and followed the Chrysler through the gates of Garden Cemetery.

***

THE COFFIN STOOD STARK beside the hole

prepared for it. Those of us who had followed Butchie to the graveyard stood in a semicircle, facing the box and the earthy darkness.

Reverend LaBelle spoke "from dust to dust" while a breeze freshened and cooled the crowd. Then four men in black suits and five women in black dresses stepped up to the edge of the hole.

One at a time, each man threw a clod into the grave. When they were done, each woman sacrificed a flower. They stood there, Butchie Stern's nine living children, heads bowed, some sobbing, then stepped back into the crowd.

Reverend LaBelle exhorted us all to learn from Butchie's example, to leave this place better, more Christian people, comforted by the fact that Butchie sat even now at the right hand of his Heavenly Father, a treasured and well-beloved child, home and at rest, at last.

The crowd dispersed with startling speed after that. I lingered, with an eye toward letting the traffic clear itself out before I started the Camaro.

He was standing at the foot of the coffin— a slender man in a tailored gray suit— back toward me, head bent slightly forward, in an attitude of— vigilance. Dark red hair glinted in the October sunshine.

I took a step toward him.

"Jenny!" Harry's shout carried too well from the roadside. "C'mon now— I've got business back to town."

The red-haired man didn't move; his concentration upon the casket appeared perfect.

I hesitated another second, then went to drive Harry back to town.

\*\*\*

RANDOM ACCESS OPENED around me. I

ignored the *Mail Waiting* note and went on to the main menu, from which all things proceedeth. The clock at the top of my screen read eight-oh-five.

At the selection bar, I typed < P > . Page the sysop.

*Calling Fox,* Random Access told me cheerfully. *One Moment Please.*

It was certainly no more than that before the familiar chat screen appeared. Words were already forming on his side of the line.

*...ello, Jennifer. What can I do for you?*

*Satisfy my curiosity,* I typed. *Was it you I saw at Reverend Stern's funeral today? Red hair, gray suit.*

*You have the advantage of me,* he returned. *Why didn't you introduce yourself? I'd have been happy to see you.*

I hesitated, biting my lip, before I typed, *I didn't see you until the end, and you looked pretty intent— standing at the foot of the coffin.*

*Ah,* Fox said. And didn't say anything more.

The silence stretched, blank-screened, between us. I was the one who broke it.

*Fox?*

*Yes. I'm here.*

*I— What were you doing there?* I typed.

*Not,* I thought, *that it's any business of mine.*

On Fox's side of the line a series of periods slowly appeared— "think-dots," intended to serve as placeholders while a chatter gathers his thoughts.

*........It's difficult to explain....Say that I was....fulfilling a vow.*

*A vow?* I repeated, hoping my typing didn't look as stupid as I felt.

*A vow,* Fox affirmed. *.......You're familiar with the work of Bob Dylan?*

There'd been a time when I'd lived, eaten and breathed Bob Dylan. My fingers moved of themselves, leaving me blinking at the line they had typed:

*I'll stand on your grave 'til I know you're dead.*
*Silly me,* said Fox. *Yes, that's the one.*
*Oh.*

*Masters of War,* one of the angriest and most blood-curdling anthems in the Dylan lexicon.

*You don't have to go to that much trouble,* I told Fox. *I certify Hyannis Stern dead, done, and deceased. He was dead when I checked his pulse out by the hay, and he was still dead today when I looked in the casket.*

A pause, before: *That does mean something, Jennifer. Thank you. .....I stayed until they'd filled the hole.*

*Oh,* I said again. *Is your vow fulfilled now?*
*.......Yes, I think it might be. Odd.*

The line broke— not the double-space that signaled my turn to type, but a mere single-space and then—

*Please don't think I'm running away from you, but I'm on deadline with a project and need to get back to it soon. Is there anything else I can do for you?*

*Yes,* I thought, *tell me why you wanted him dead.*

*Thank you, no,* my fingers typed politely. *I didn't mean to disturb your work.*

*It's no trouble. I enjoy chatting with you,* Fox said. *Call again?*

I smiled, absurdly warmed. *Unless you lock me out.*
*Highly unlikely. Good night, Jennifer.*
*Good night, Fox.*

Random Access bloomed around me.

# 18

THURSDAY. THE SKY WAS a pewter bowl, sullen and threatening rain. Cat on my knee, I ate toast and drank coffee, then drove downtown to do errands.

I came out of Dore's Hardware carrying the roll of plastic that represented, according to Alvie Dore, the least amount I would need to "winterize"— read, "cover with plastic sheeting"— the first floor windows in Aunt Jen's house. It seemed to me that the roll had been smaller, last year, but I do tend to trivialize Herculean undertakings, in retrospect.

"Hi, Jenny."

The voice came from my right. I checked my stride to look up at Craig.

"Hi."

He smiled. "You off today?"

"I work tonight," I said grudgingly. "I'm running errands."

"Hey, sure." His smile widened. "Want me to carry that for you?"

The roll was heavy— the bum left shoulder was already yelling for its shop steward— and I would have rather died on the spot than admit I needed help.

"No, thanks." I lengthened my stride, teeth set.

"Okay," Craig said. He kept pace easily, hands tucked into the pockets of his denim jacket. "So, what're you doing tomorrow night?"

Tomorrow night? What did I do every night I wasn't working? I read, listened to music— and surfed the boards from Maine to Mexico.

"Nothing," I told Craig between gritted teeth and paused at the curb before crossing Main Street to the Camaro.

"Hey, that's great. I'll pick you up at six."

I bent and let the plastic roll slide butt first out of my arms to the sidewalk. I leaned it carefully against the Camaro's back quarter-panel, then straightened and looked at Craig.

"You'll do what?"

"I'll pick you up at six," he repeated blithely. "You like Chinese? I figure we can do the Jade Dragon for dinner and catch the late movie over in Waterville. Okay?"

My temper is erratic, not gentle. My character, despite years of rigorous training designed to make it so, is neither placid nor pliant.

I took a deep breath. "No."

Craig didn't even blink. "Don't like Chinese? No problem. We can do—"

"No. We. Can't." I interrupted, in a voice that would have sent the White Sheep scrambling for cover in the old days of shared bedrooms.

It gave Craig pause. He looked at me, brows drawn together in puzzlement. "What?"

"I said, 'Thank you, Craig, but I don't want to go out with you tomorrow night.'" *Or any other night in this lifetime,* I added silently. The memory of his face when I'd refused to kiss him was still vivid. No way was I going to get involved with that. Whatever it was.

Craig was actively frowning now. "Why not?"

*Because you're shallow, dim, and under certain I hope really specialized circumstances, scary as hell.* "I don't date."

"You don't date." The intensity of the sarcasm startled me. I hadn't thought he had that much depth. He leaned forward, almost in my face.

"You mean you don't date me."

"All right," I said equitably. "If you will have it: I don't date you. Happy now?"

That was a mistake.

His hand shot out, gripped my left shoulder, fingers like bands of iron, tightening. I gasped; he yanked me forward.

"You got a hell of a mouth on you for a scrawny bitch."

My shoulder. He was going to break my shoulder. I could hear the bones grinding together.

"Then it's no loss," I panted, squinting at him through tears of pain, "if I won't— go out with you."

He glared, fingers tightening. I wondered if I would black out when the break came and if anybody had called the cops yet. This was for God's sake Main Street. What the hell did people think was going on here?

Craig's face twisted. "Why the— "

"Hey!" The voice was clear, outraged and entirely familiar.

"What the hell's going on here?" demanded Merry Ash.

Craig's grip slackened and he turned his head to stare at this new aggravation. I glimpsed Merry beyond him, hands on her hips, face paper-white under the absurd platinum curls: a pint-sized avenger.

"None of your business," Craig snarled.

Merry's face changed. I am not prepared to say exactly how it changed— perhaps it went from anger to... detachment.

"It's my business now," she said, and her voice had changed, too, taken on timbre— authority. "Let her go."

Craig's fingers loosened a bit more— from sheer

amazement, most likely. I took a careful breath, willing myself to stand perfectly still and wait for it.

"This is between me and Jenny," Craig said, and jerked his head to the left. "Get lost."

Merry shook her head. "Think you can get away with anything, don't you?" she asked, conversationally. "Think you can get away with roughing up a woman on Main Street. Think you can get away with the whole ball of wax. Think nothing'll ever go wrong. Think nobody'll ever look at you and know you for what you are." She shook her head again. "Your days of luck are numbered, friend. Look at me and believe it."

As theater, it was beautiful. Rational discourse, it was not. Either way, it was arresting— even disturbing. Craig went back a step, fingers releasing that last necessary fraction of pressure.

I yanked myself free, twisting away and down, swung around hard and came up straight beside Merry Ash, who was watching the whole thing with wide, half-dazed eyes.

"Get the hell out of here!" I shouted at Craig.

He seemed to shake himself; actually tried a smile. I shuddered, ears buzzing with adrenaline.

"C'mon, Jenny. It was a joke."

I swallowed. "You get out of here now," I said, voice thin but steady, "and I'll only call Morris. You stand there one minute more and I'm calling the cops."

It didn't take him a minute to decide. He shrugged— "Okay. If that's how you want it."— turned and crossed the street, heading uptown with a long, unhurried stride.

I let my breath out with a whoosh. Beside me, Merry Ash said, "You should have called the cops."

I looked down at her. Rage and calm detachment were likewise gone from her face. She looked exhausted and as shaky as I felt.

"Got a phone on you?" I asked, and my voice was shaking, too.

"Nah..." The word came out as a sigh. It took me a second to realize she was trying to smile. She raised a hand that was none too steady and ran it through her hair. The silver wedding band shimmered against the dim air.

"I hate when that happens," she said, and I don't think she meant assaults on Main Street.

"You were right on cue," I told her and pointed at the car. "I don't know about you, but I've got to sit down. You're welcome to the passenger seat."

"Good idea."

\*\*\*

"I WENT TO SEE SCOTT," Merry said, her head against the high back of the bucket seat, staring up through the sunroof. "He's in bad shape— hates being cooped up. Always has. Feels like he should've done something about your boyfriend there when he saw him come in. Might've saved Reverend Slime's life, kept himself out of jail." She sighed and closed her eyes.

"In a fair way to believing he *deserves* to be in jail, because a man who fails to prevent a murder is just as guilty as the man who does the deed."

"That sounds Roman Catholic," I commented around the acrid taste of left-over adrenaline. "Not Wiccan."

She snorted and opened her eyes. "Yeah, well."

We were quiet for a little while. The worst of the shaking had eased off, leaving me feeling drained and light-headed. I sighed, looking out the windshield at Wimsy Main Street. There were maybe six people, up and down the walk.

Thursday morning. Scott had been arrested on Monday.

"You got a lawyer yet?" I asked Merry.

Her mouth tightened and she continued to stare at, if not through, the sunroof. "Lawyer," she repeated. I saw her throat work.

"We sunk everything we had into that farm," she said. "All the years of saving up and following the work..." She sighed. "We own the place. But lawyers don't want to get paid in sheep."

"Maybe in Maine," I suggested, "they still do."

She hiccupped, halfway between a laugh and a sob, I think, then shook her head. "Have to mortgage the farm, isn't that what they say up here?" She closed her eyes, face twisting. "But, yeah. We've got a lawyer. Much good as he's done."

I bit my tongue. After a minute, I asked, "Does Scott think Craig killed Reverend Stern?"

Merry sighed. "Scott's not thinking too good right now." Finally, she turned to look at me. "You ought to file a complaint against that guy. Really. Guys who like to hurt women don't just stop because they didn't get their thrill this time."

She was right, of course. And a complaint on file would help the cops, if something ugly happened again. Which is called "cold comfort," even in Maine.

I flexed my shoulder— wasn't quite able to stifle the gasp. "Oh. Wow." Bad, bad. Really bad. It hadn't hurt like this since the beginning of physical therapy....

"He hurt you?" Merry demanded.

Closing my eyes, I sat entirely still, waiting for the worst of it to ease. When I thought my voice could be trusted, I opened my eyes.

"Bum shoulder from— a car crash. Couple years back. That's the shoulder he grabbed."

"Bastard."

"Yeah..." I sighed. "I think I will file that complaint. Then I'll have a talk with Morris."

"Good idea." She straightened in the passenger's seat. "We can go over to the police station right now." She flicked me a glance. "Get it over with."

"No time like the present," I agreed, fumbling the key ring out of my jacket pocket. I paused with the ignition key half-inserted. "Hell. I forgot about that damn plastic."

"I'll get it," Merry said, popping the door. "Chuck it in the trunk for you?"

"Thanks." I said, and handed her the keys. "I'd appreciate that."

*** 

EASY-GOING JOHN Therriault took the complaint.

"Morris DuChamp's new hand," he repeated tonelessly, looking as stern as I've ever seen him.

I nodded.

"Okay," he, glancing down at the desk and the scribbled sheets of paper there. He shook his head and looked back to me.

"There's a couple things we can do," he said. "I can summons him— means it would go to trial and you and Mrs. Ash would testify— tell—the judge what you told me." He looked at me closely. "You willing to testify against this fella, Jenny?"

I stared at him, feeling my shoulder shriek and burn while I remembered—

I hadn't known her well. We happened to work at adjoining desks in the steno pool. Sometimes, when our schedules matched, we ate lunch together and told over the shortcomings of our co-workers. Angie, her name had been. She was dating a guy named Rick.

One evening while he was a wee bit tipsy Rick smacked Angie into a wall and broke her arm. She filed a complaint— and took him to court. Testified against him, despite at least one threat that Rick would "break every bone in her body" unless she dropped charges.

Unfortunately, Rick's lawyer had been the better of the two. Rick walked. Angie changed the locks on the apartment, made sure she always left work and went to her car with another girl or three from the pool— stratagems that worked for about a week, I guess.

He caught her one Saturday morning in the apartment's basement laundry room, and if he didn't break every bone in her body, well, no one could say that he hadn't tried.

I drew a careful breath, feeling kind of tight in the chest, shoulder burning; cleared my throat and said, "What's Plan B?"

John sighed. "I can go on over and have a talk with him, check his ID— put some of the fear of God into him." His mouth tightened. "That works— sometimes."

It was still risky, and Craig.... But, dammit, I'd started this. I'd already chickened out of the really tough one. If I was totally spineless, I preferred to learn it some other day. And maybe a good, stern cop-sermon was just what Craig needed. Maybe.

I looked at John. "Okay," I said, "go ahead and put the fear of God into him."

*\*\*\**

BACK HOME, I SCRAMBLED the bottle of pills out of the medicine cabinet, downed two— one too many, according to the dosage instructions from the doctor— then put the bottle away and unbuttoned my shirt.

In the mirror, the skin showed a point of angry red— where Craig's thumb would have been, I thought. Other colors were beginning to show themselves: Purple. Green. Yellow.

Terrific.

Bracing myself, I slowly raised my arm until my fingers touched the low bathroom ceiling. It felt bad, don't doubt it— but the shoulder worked. I was only bruised.

Carefully, I lowered the arm, buttoned my blouse, splashed cold water on my face and combed my hair.

Thus armored against adversity, I went to phone Morris.

# 19

MORRIS' LINE RANG EMPTY.

I went down to the kitchen, made myself some coffee and a tuna fish sandwich, replenished Jasper's rations. About halfway through the sandwich the drug hit— a bones-melting-inside-your-flesh kind of feeling that should have been terrifying, but wasn't, because my brain had melted first.

I sagged in the chair and called down blessings upon Upjohn Company, its subsidiaries and properties, which I would not do in about ten hours, when I had the shakes and the heebie-jeebies, but why think about the future? Surcease from the pain was what mattered in the present, and that I most gratefully had.

I blinked affectionately at the sandwich wedge in my hand. Upon reflection, it was very likely the best tuna fish sandwich I'd had so far this century and I savored it as it deserved, thoroughly chewing every bite.

Finished at last, I cleared the table, putting the sandwich plate into the sink and warming my coffee from the pot on the counter. I put the mug on the table and went through the swinging door into the dining room, thence to the parlor, and my auxiliary library.

Aunt Jen had left a fair collection of books behind her. Indeed, one whole wall of the parlor was sacrificed to floor-to-ceiling bookshelves, which, judging from the well-thumbed appearance of the carpentry manuals, she may have built herself. When my own books overflowed the inadequate quarters I had built for them in my room, it had seemed reasonable and just that they come to roost here.

It took a few minutes, in my muzzy-headed state, to locate the particular book I wanted. I found it at last near the bottom right, nestled cozily against an illustrated *Midsummer's Night Dream*, hefted it and took it with me back to the kitchen.

Seated at the table, coffee at my right hand, I blinked bemusedly at the heavy cardboard cover and its formidable black letters: *The Mercenary Soldier's Survival Guide*, which text devoted one very detailed chapter to Plain and Fancy Killing.

This may seem an odd book for a maiden-secretary-turned-reporter to have in her private collection. My reading habits have always been eclectic, not to say voracious, and, as a citizen of a city rich in bookstores, I'd been able to indulge my whim to the fullest. I'd once owned a copy of *The Anarchist's Cookbook*. My ex-husband took it with him when he left.

I opened the *Guide* and laboriously perused the table of contents. My subject was discussed in chapter eight. I riffled the pages to the beginning of the chapter and paused to have a sip of coffee and try to focus my melted brain.

It wasn't easy, but I managed to buckle down on the narrative— and was abruptly thankful for the drug, which was blunting reality very nicely, thank you, and making it difficult to recall that these were proven techniques to bring about human deaths we were talking about here.

I hadn't liked Hyannis Stern and I disagreed vehemently with the principle he had made the touchstone of his life. But he had been a person, with the total of his allotted time already written at the bottom of his dance card. *No one*, save Butchie himself, had the right to check him out early.

Except that someone had found it expedient or necessary to do so.

I shook my head, and the words suddenly leaped out at me, seeming to etch themselves in the air several inches above the page:

*A silent and difficult-to-detect kill, ideal for situations where stealth is of the essence. Drawbacks include necessary extreme proximity to the target. Most useful in situations where the agent is well-known to the target. Materials needed: piano wire, or: hat pin, ice pick. Piano wire recommended as easiest to conceal.*

*The strike is made to the solar plexus, to a depth of one-half inch only. Heart action terminates immediately, death following within seconds....* I closed my eyes, which was a mistake, because then I could see Butchie Stern even plainer, lying dead and peaceful on the grass.

*You just have to know where to hit, that's all,* Merry Ash told me bleakly from memory. *Human beings are really pretty fragile.*

I opened my eyes, and looked back at the page. There was a bit more of the same, mostly concerned with technicalities. I can't say it registered— though the discussion must have been interesting to someone possessing professional skill.

Someone like Scott Ash, who, according to the cops and according to his wife, possessed such professional skill in quantity sufficient to the task.

I flipped the book closed and lay my head on top of the cover. The paper was grainy against my cheek; the book smelled like dust. I sneezed.

A puttery puff of a purr sounded from the vicinity of my lap: I'd been so intent on the *Guide* that I hadn't noticed Jasper jumping up. Closing my eyes, I sighed and put my hand blindly along his fur. The purr solidified, took on volume. After a while, the clinging dust initiated another sneeze and I raised my head. The clock over the refrigerator read five-thirty.

"Time to go to work, cat," I said, and moved my legs carefully. Jasper jumped down and went over to inspect his water dish. I got up, poured cold coffee down the drain, and took my jacket off its peg.

\*\*\*

WORK WAS A DISASTER.

I fumbled an obit and had to call the director back for a rematch. She was not amused, and didn't try to hide it. I *hate* being told I'm incompetent.

Especially when it's true.

Steaming, I patched the obit, proofed and sent it, then dug into my notes on Willard Quirion, who had just opened a truck detailing shop down River Road. It had been a difficult interview, Willard not being a particularly talkative fella. We were also hampered by his stated philosophy that talking trucks to a girl was as bootless as teaching a pig to sing— and not nearly so much fun. Nor did the Camaro impress him. Willard was a truck man, bone and blood. Pissant little go-cars were for girls. Or fags.

Across such a gulf, communication necessarily faltered. I was as little pleased with my notes as I was with Willard and I had put off writing the thing for an entire week. Tonight, according to Bill Jacques, there was a Willard-sized hole on the business page, and it had my name on it.

I marshaled my diminished forces and dug in, finding a lead with an ease that would have set off mental alarm bells if my skull hadn't been stuffed with cotton batting. As it was, it nagged at me a little, but, working on the theory that a lead is better than no lead, I persevered until I had wrung a healthy twelve inches out of Willard and The Truck Farm.

With a sense of profound relief, I proofed the thing, ran the spell-checker, coded, copied and sent it.

"Trucks-point-Jen coming across," I called into the general clatter.

"Got it!" Carly the copy editor sang out and I gathered my stuff for the nightly check-in at the police station.

I was almost out the door when Carly called me.

"Jen? You got a second?"

"Sure." I walked over to her desk and stood beside the monitor, facing her as she faced the screen. "Question?"

"Well..." she said, with a certain un-Carly-like hesitation. She tapped the screen. "Is this lead right?"

I moved behind her chair and frowned at the grainy yellow letters wavering on the screen: *Willard Quirion is a big man with a big ego— and he loves big trucks.*

"Well," I said slowly, "it's accurate."

"Oh," said Carly, somewhat dubiously. There followed a beat of five before she said, brightly, "I'll just take out the ego part, okay?"

"Sure," I agreed, swallowing against the panic rising in my chest. Had I written that lead? Really? I must be more doped up than I knew. I cleared my throat.

"I'm going over to get the cop log," I told Carly. "Be back in fifteen minutes, if you find something else."

"Okay."

Notebook gripped tight, I fled.

\*\*\*

The log was longish and Night Sergeant Ken Aube was in a mood to share gossip, so it was closer to forty-five minutes later before I regained the newsroom. Bill Jacques looked up as I came through the door and crooked a finger.

I approached him with trepidation.

"Problem?" I asked.

He crossed his arms on top the monitor and grinned. "Willard get under your skin?"

Oh-oh. "That bad, huh? I'll do a rewrite."

"Already did one," he said softly. "Cost you five bucks on the story, though. Byline's now 'Staff.'"

I exhaled. "Thank you."

He cocked an eyebrow. "He really got to you."

"Oh, the man's a redneck," I said, with an unexpected rush of feeling.

"Come up in the puckerbrush," Bill agreed, and looked at me sharply. "You okay?"

"Yeah, I'm okay. Tired."

He nodded and unfolded his arms. "Send me the cop log, then get the hell outta here. Go home and get some rest. I don't want to ever see another Willard from you, understand?"

I saluted, trying for jaunty. I don't think I made it. "Yessir."

Bill's eyes were already back on his screen. "Dismissed."

I went back to Karen's Desk and flipped open my notebook.

\*\*\*

IT LACKED A COUPLE minutes to eleven when I eased the Camaro out of the *Voice's* lot and onto Main Street. LaVerdiere's and Dore's Hardware were dark when I glided past; a security light bathed Mother's Pantry in pale shadow. Above, the sky was sullen with cloud: no stars, no moon.

I turned right onto Preble Street and flicked the radio

on, catching the unmistakable nasal whine of Bob Dylan's voice:

*Come you masters of war...*

I shivered, though it was warm inside the Camaro, then reached down to turn the volume up.

Mind on the song, I drove automatically, going west on the Stone Road, waiting— almost dreading— that last angry verse.

Fox. Fox and his damned vow. People didn't vow anymore. People hadn't vowed for a hundred years— didn't he know that? I took a hard breath. How much did you have to hate somebody, to wish them so— emphatically— dead?

Dylan's voice continued, implacably, coldly savage. I negotiated the slight rise and turn in the road— and blinked.

There was something— odd— about the sky.

Before me, set off slightly to the left, the sky was— flickering.

I reached down and snapped the radio off.

"For pity's sake, Jen," I scolded myself. "It's only an aurora."

Auroras are common enough in Central Maine. On clear nights.

"Something's on fire," I told myself, and turned onto the Point Road.

The fire was closer now— I could see the outlines of flames etched against the sullen sky.

*Oh, no.*

The Johnson— Ash— place was the first drive on my right. Heart in mouth, I guided the Camaro in, going down the rutted lane with an alacrity that paid no respect to shock absorbers.

The dooryard was strobe-lit by the manic orange

flames engulfing the barn. I slammed on the brakes and was running for the house before I had time to see more than that.

Merry Ash met me halfway: bathrobe. Bare feet.

"Fire Department!" I yelled.

"Did that," she yelled back, and grabbed my sleeve, yanking me with her toward the barn. "We've gotta get the animals out!"

## 20

I'VE NEVER HAD MUCH respect for sheep.

They were terrified— even a sheep has that much sense— milling around the pen, bumbling into each other. They might even have been screaming sheep screams, but I didn't hear them. The roar of the fire filled up my ears.

Merry twisted the hem of her robe round her hand, worked the metal latch and swung the gate wide. Anticipating a stampede, I stepped back. The air was hot and sanded with soot. Somewhere overhead, a beam broke with a shriek; sparks swirled like snowflakes from hell.

And the sheep— Just. Stood. There.

Merry was in the pen, pushing at sheep, slapping the rumps of sheep. The fire roared louder still. On the wall beside me, a coil of rope exploded into flame.

"Shit! Merry! Get out of there!" I flung into the pen, screaming, but the fire smothered my voice. Dozens of inert woolly bodies were blocking my way and Merry was going to *die* and: "The barn's afire, you stupid animals!"

The sheep directly before me wore a collar with a bell attached. I grabbed it and yanked, digging my heels in and yelling curses into the blazing roar. The sheep stayed put.

I yanked again, two-handed, then let go to use both hands and all my strength to smack the fat woolly rump.

A miracle occurred.

The sheep moved.

And all the other sheep moved, following the one I had just pasted, to the open gate, through it....

The leader hesitated in the open barn, looking from

side to side. I pushed and shoved my way to the front of the line, grabbed the collar and hauled her head toward the door, then went behind and whaled her again.

It worked.

They broke into a run as they came into the yard. Merry had made it out of the pen by then. I grabbed her and half-dragged, half-carried her out into the crazy-quilt night.

Once they warm up to the notion, sheep run pretty fast. We stood there, leaning against each other and watching them go, through the kitchen garden, around the pond and off into the next field.

"Can't go far," Merry panted. "I think."

Which was about the time Wimsy Volunteer Fire Department began to arrive.

\*\*\*

IT TOOK THREE PUMP trucks— both of Wimsy's engines and one from Waterville— to contain the inferno. Along about two a.m., Chief Bob Giles stepped up to talk to Merry.

"She'll smolder for awhile," he said, jerking his head at the steaming wreckage. "Might be two, three days. We'll keep a couple fellas here with the pond pump for a few hours, just to see she don't flare up again. Can't be too careful." He sighed. "Good thing you got the animals out."

Merry nodded without moving her eyes from the barn. Tin roofing had peeled in sheets and fallen through the flame-rotted roof. They lay like nightmare sculpture amid the ashes. Sections of wall nearly as tall as I am and truncated support beams still stood, but most of what was left was rubble— black, smoking and forbidding.

Bob glanced at me, clearly troubled. "Might be a good

idea for you ladies to get some rest. Jerry went up the road to turn the 'lectric back on."

I nodded, and decided against trying to smile. "That's a good idea. Thanks— you guys got here really fast."

That helped a little. He ducked his head bashfully. "Do our best."

"You did great," I told him, sincerely. "It never got near the house." The Waterville truck had been hosing down the roof pretty constantly to prevent just that leap of faith on the part of the fire. I hoped the Ash's attic wasn't full of water as a result.

Bob looked pleased. "I'll tell the fellas you said so, Miz Pierce. Means a lot to hear some thanks."

Beside me, Merry shivered, but said nothing. Bob stood with us another minute, then nodded good-morning and went away.

I touched Merry's shoulder. "Time to go in and wash up," I said. "Maybe take a nap."

For a heartbeat, there was no response. She was out on her feet, I thought, and who could blame her? I was ready to fall flat, myself, and the two mile drive to my own house and bed loomed like a labor of Hercules.

"Right," Merry said then, scratchy voiced. "C'mon in. You can have the couch."

Under normal conditions, I don't sleep in other people's houses. However, conditions had been stripped of normalcy some hours back.

"Thanks," I said, and turned with her toward the house.

We'd gone about four steps when she passed out.

\*\*\*

I FOLLOWED THE RESCUE across the river to

Waterville Hospital, and sat in the empty waiting room, staring at nothing.

I'd tried cleaning myself up in the ladies room, with minimal success. Soot is a remarkably tenacious substance. Once, a nurse came by and asked if I wanted coffee. I did.

Mostly, though, I sat, not really listening to the canned music or sporadic calls for this doctor or that nurse; not really thinking: asleep with my eyes open, I guess.

Finally, someone came by— it might have been the same nurse— and asked if I was Merry Ash's sister.

I made an effort to sit up straight. "Just a friend," I muttered. "Was with her when her barn burned."

The nurse nodded, unsurprised and uncurious. "You can go home now and get some rest," she said. "We're going to keep your friend for observation."

This did not sound good.

"Observation. What's wrong with her?"

The nurse frowned.

"Look," I said, "her husband's in jail, and her nearest kin, if she has any, is in Massachusetts. If it's a privacy problem, we can just pretend I told you I *was* her sister."

The frown flickered; became a smile.

"All right. It's nothing awful— we just like to be careful. It looks like your friend fainted because her blood sugar went too low— hypoglycemia. We'd want to make sure she's stable before we sent her home. Also...." She paused, then gave a tiny shrug. "She might be in the very early stages of pregnancy." She smiled again, professionally, and reached over to pat my hand.

"You look dead on your feet. Go on home and get some rest, okay? Your friend's going to be just fine."

"Okay," I said. I reached into my pocketbook, pulled out my notebook, scrawled my name and phone number on a clean sheet and tore it out. "Call me," I said, "if something happens. Okay?"

She took the paper and put it in her pocket.

"Okay." She rose. "Go home."

"Going now."

I remember walking across the waiting room and out into the dawn. I remember finding the Camaro and getting in.

It must have driven itself home.

\*\*\*

I DREAMED I WAS DROWNING, pinned under water by the weight of the boulder on my chest. I woke, gasping for breath, but the weight on my chest was undiminished. Panting, I wrenched my eyes open.

Jasper lay on my chest, paws neatly together under his chin, eyes squinted in pleasure. He was purring: I could feel it, deep in the cavity of my chest. I let out my breath in a *pouf*; Jasper flicked an ear, but continued to purr.

"You weigh too much, cat," I told him. The purrs increased in volume. I sighed and lifted a tentative finger. Jasper touched it with his nose; I moved my hand and did a little gentle skritching along the side of his jaw.

The purrs echoed pleasantly inside my chest. I closed my eyes, skritching and half-dozing, until Jasper gently moved his head, rose, stretched with a certain sensual elegance and jumped off the bed.

I turned my head and squinted at the clock: ten-thirty. A little light mental wrestling produced the fact that I'd had all of four hours' sleep, but I wasn't inclined to turn over for another four. In fact, now that it had been kicked into action, my brain was busily compiling a long list of things that It Would Be Good For Jen To Do Today.

So be it.

My shoulder grabbed as I flung the covers back and I swore. The pain hardly outlived the curse, but I got up carefully and stretched both hands high over my head. Ouch.

"Cranky but functional," I reported to Jasper, who was sitting on top the vanity, and lowered my arms. "Life goes on."

\*\*\*

THE REMAINS OF THE BARN looked worse in the full light of morning: black and soggy and subtly threatening. I got out of the Camaro and stood looking at the ruins, nose wrinkled against the stink of stale smoke.

All in all, a thorough job, I decided. It was a good thing that the old Johnson place hadn't been built along the lines of a "regular" Maine house. A fire like that would have been up the ell in seconds, devouring the house in minutes.

I turned away, crossing the yard in a couple strides. There was no sign of the sheep, but the brown cat was sitting on the porch, four variously colored kittens napping nearby.

Mom rose when she saw me, and issued a very explicit set of instructions as I mounted the steps.

"Right," I said. "Milk, mouse and tuna. I'll see what I can do." I bent down and offered a forefinger. She acknowledged the introduction with a dainty touch of her cheek, then settled back on her haunches.

The door was unlocked. Of course. I let myself in, ran water into a couple saucers and carried them outside. There was a box of dry cat food in the pantry. I filled a couple more saucers and carried them out, whereupon Mom deigned to inspect and approve my choices. Under her watchful eye, the kittens set to, and I was released to my original purpose.

The bedroom was upstairs; the single large window facing the fields behind the house. The furniture was heavy— old-fashioned dark wood: bed, wardrobe and chest. Framed photo on the chest: Scott and Merry encircled by men and women in brightly colored, monklike robes. The sun was brilliant, the grass green and endless. There were flowers all around. Scott was wearing loose trousers and a wide-sleeved shirt, soft-looking boots on his feet, a wreath of flowers around his neck. Merry was in a long green dress, cut low over her breasts— barefoot; flowers in her hair. They were holding hands, smiling. Glowing.

I stared at the photo, ensorcelled by the image of their happiness. My own wedding had been a furtive thing— five minutes at City Hall and a dry proclamation by a gray-suited man who'd forgotten our names before it came time to write them down. No flowers. No circle of happy friends to share the joy of joining two lives together.

"It was a long time ago, Jen," I told myself and turned away at last.

I found jeans, underwear and socks in the enormous chest of drawers, and piled them neatly on the bed. The wardrobe yielded a green sweatshirt. I added that to the pile with a pair of comfortably battered sneakers.

Further search did not produce a suitcase, so I carried my booty downstairs and packed it all neatly into a brown grocery bag before going on my way, shutting the door firmly behind me.

The kittens were lolling about in the sun, bellies distended. Mom was knoshing crunchies, but she looked up politely as I went by and called a companionable, "Neow!"

"No problem," I told her.

I put the bag on the passenger's seat, webbed into the driver's side, put the Camaro into gear and headed for Waterville.

# 21

"MERRY ASH? JUST A moment." The receptionist tapped a quick code into her keyboard, frowning at the terminal. The frown deepened and she picked up a light-pen to make three quick stabs at the screen.

"I'm sorry," she said then, "Mrs. Ash has asked not to be disturbed."

"She has?" I worried at that for a second. "Is she admitted, or— "

She glanced at her screen. "Under observation," she said, cutting me off.

"Still?" I asked. "The nurse last night said it was no big deal."

The receptionist shrugged. "It probably isn't. But she came in at three-thirty *this morning*, not last night. They like to keep them eight to twelve hours for observation." She smiled, suddenly friendly. "Nothing to worry about yet. She probably put up the do not disturb sign so she could get some sleep."

"Oh." I showed her the paper bag. "I brought her some clothes."

"No problem," she said. "You can leave the bag with me, if you want, and I'll have it taken up to her."

It would have to do. "Sure. Let me just write a note." I scrawled my number and Harry Pelletier's on a sheet torn from my notebook, with the instructions: "Call me if you need a ride. If I'm not around, Harry will come and get you. Jen." I put the note in the bag, re-rolled the top and shoved it across the counter to the receptionist.

"Thanks."

"No problem," she said again, putting the bag on the corner of her desk. "I'll have somebody take this up, okay? In the meantime, try checking back around two."

"Right."

I stopped at the pay phones on my way out, dumped in a quarter and punched up the number. Harry answered on the second ring.

"Yep."

"Harry, it's Jen— you going to be around today?"

"Mostly."

"Do me a favor, will you? Merry Ash is at Waterville Hospital. They figure they'll let her out sometime around two or three o'clock. Can you give her a ride home if she calls you?"

"Can do that."

"Thanks, Harry. See you later."

"You bet." The connection went dead.

Grinning, I hung up the phone and got out of there.

\*\*\*

KENNEBEC COUNTY Correctional Facility is located at 115 State Street in Augusta, Maine, and looks like nothing so much as the Disneyland Castle's evil, brooding twin.

I parked by the district court building, and walked the block or so to the jail, frowning at the various gray stone facades. When I came to the facade that interested me most, I went down the short entry walk, up the steps and through the wide glass door.

\*\*\*

SCOTT WAS PALER THAN he'd been a week ago.
He stared at me blankly through the thick glass, then shook
his head, a frown creasing his forehead.

"What do you want?"

"To let you know what's happened," I said. "I'm here
as a friend, Scott. Not for the paper."

"Friend." He said the word like it was something
foreign— sound without meaning.

"Friend," I repeated firmly. "Listen, your barn burned
down last night. The sheep got out— even the cats got out.
But the barn's totaled. I'm sorry."

His face lost a little more color; his eyes remained
fixed on mine.

"Where's Merry?" he asked then. "Why are you here?"

It was an effort to keep my gaze on his, but I did it.

"Merry's under observation at Waterville Hospital," I
told him, not even trying for tact, which I have never had.
"She fainted. The doctors think low blood sugar, and they
don't want to let her go until they're sure she's not going to
faint again the minute she gets home." I omitted the other
possibility mentioned by the night nurse. Let Merry break
that news, if there was that news to break.

Scott's eyes went wide, he leaned forward, eyes boring
into mine. "Merry's sick?" He leaned back suddenly, lifting
his hand to run the hair back off his forehead.

"They've got to let me out of here," he said, voice fast
and low. "I tell them and tell them I didn't do it— they don't
listen— and now Merry's sick and the barn's down— Dammit,
I need to go home!" This last went dangerously loud. The cop
by the door moved.

"Lower your voice," he said, flat-voiced himself. Scott
flicked him a blazing glare, then looked back to me, leaning
forward and muttering into the grate.

"You've got to get me out of here," he said, as if I could. "You say you're my friend— *Merry's* friend. Get me out. Make them listen."

I stared; felt my mouth open, though I had no idea what I could possibly say until I heard the words, and my own voice, ridiculously calm:

"I'll do what I can."

"Time," said the cop by the door, and came forward to take Scott's arm.

\*\*\*

BRUCE GAGNON WASN'T in, which I suppose was just as well. I returned to the Camaro, started it up, and pulled out into Augusta midday traffic.

*Of all the simple-minded promises to make!* I scolded myself as I passed the YMCA. *As if there's anything at all you can do to get Scott Ash out of jail. That's why he has a lawyer. You're not a lawyer, Jennifer. You're not even a detective. You're a half-baked reporter with a severe attitude problem. There is nothing you can do for Scott Ash. Nothing!*

By the time I cleared city limits, I'd thought of something.

\*\*\*

"MERRY ASH?" THIS WAS a different receptionist— an elderly man with disapproving brown eyes. They frowned at me over the top of his half-glasses. "You're a relative?"

"A friend," I said, determinedly cheerful. "She was going to be released this afternoon and I thought she might need a ride home."

He sniffed— "Just a moment"— and tapped a peevish sequence into his keyboard. After a minute, he hrrmphed and looked back at me.

"Merry Ash has checked out," he told me, and pointedly looked down at the mail he'd been sorting when I'd come in.

I gritted my teeth. "Thank you," I said in my perkiest, cheeriest voice. "Have a nice day!" He didn't even look up.

The elevator bank was to my left. I exited stage that-way and pressed the up-button. Doors slid open immediately. I stepped into the cage and touched "4."

The doors whispered closed and the elevator began to rise.

*** 

"JACQUELINE STERN?" This receptionist was in fact a nurse. She looked at me, puzzled, but willing to play. "May I have your name?"

"Jennifer Pierce," I said calmly, and then, in a subdued voice. "I knew her husband."

"Oh." The nurse blinked, reached down and touched her keypad; brought up the lightpen and flicked it twice at the screen.

"Mrs. Stern is allowed single visitors for up to fifteen minutes," she said, eyes on the screen. "Room six-ay." She sheathed the lightpen and looked up at me. "Straight down that hall, on the right."

"Thanks."

She nodded. "Fifteen minutes, remember."

"I'll remember," I promised and went down the hall.

The door to 6A was ajar. I hesitated, then knocked lightly.

"Come in!" A cheery voice called. I obeyed, pushing the door almost to behind me.

It was a hospital room, painfully tidy, as hospital rooms tend to be. The bed was made within an inch of its life. Two chairs sat by the window overlooking the parking lot. One was occupied.

"Come in, come in!" The cheery voice called again. "Closer, child— don't be shy."

I went forward, half-blinded by the glare, and stood looking down at a buxom white-haired lady in a neat navy dress. Her face was round, wrinkled like a winter apple. Her eyes were almost colorless, as if time had faded them. Maybe they had once been blue.

"Well, now!" She smiled broadly. "I don't think I know you at all." She held out a soft, liver-spotted hand. "I'm Jackie Stern."

"Jennifer Pierce." Her hand was cool, her grip light— an old-fashioned "lady's shake." My grandmother had shaken hands like this.

"Jennifer Pierce," she mused, releasing me and folding her hands neatly in her lap. A smile lit her face. "Why, you're the clever child who writes for the paper! I do *so* enjoy your stories. The piece you did on the funeral quite had me in whoops! I wasn't supposed to have seen it, of course, but the staff is so careless. Allow me to congratulate you, my dear. You have the touch."

*Fourth floor's for mental cases, Jen,* I reminded myself and smiled down at her. "Thank you. Always nice to meet a fan."

"Praise is wine for an artist's ear," she said wisely, and smoothed her skirt. "But you came to see me, and I know they won't let you stay long. What can I do for you?"

This was going to be tricky. On the drive in from

Augusta, I'd convinced myself that of course Butchie's wife would have some notion of who could have wished him harm. Now, faced with the reality of her, I wasn't so sure.

*Might as well ask the question, Jen.*

I cleared my throat. "Well, I— I was wondering if they had told you, Mrs. Stern— "

She held up a hand. "Jackie. I insist."

"— Jackie. I was wondering if they had told you that your husband didn't die of natural causes. He was murdered."

Jackie clapped her hands like a delighted child and laughed. It was a pretty laugh, really. Like bells.

"Oh, but how perfectly wonderful! Of course! I knew he would do it, in the end! Such a clever, clever boy! And so *very* angry." She leaned forward in her chair, voice dropping to a confidential murmur.

"Do you know, I had quite despaired of him? Why, who could blame me? It had been *such* a long time— three years? four years?— not really long, of course, when one gets to be my age, but the young are so— precipitous, don't you find?"

I stared at her. After a moment, she smiled and flipped a coquettish hand. "Why, you're nothing but a baby yourself! I fancy you think three years an *enormous* amount of time to wait on revenge!"

I took a very, very careful breath. *She's crazy, Jen. Remember that.*

"Excuse me, Mrs.— Jackie. Are you telling me you know who killed Reverend Stern?"

She went still, then leaned back in her chair. "Well. Know. Naturally, one *hopes*. I had been so certain of him. Really, I almost felt he would do it before the trial was over— though of course, that would hardly have been clever and he truly *was* a clever boy." She sighed, smiling with grandmotherly pride. "Such eyes! I remember him, sitting in the courtroom, staring at Hyannis..." Another sigh, pure bliss. "Oh, but how those eyes could *hate!*"

I cleared my throat. "Hate— why?"

She looked at me in bright surprise. "Why? Oh, but you weren't there— how silly of me to be forgetting! My memory is not at all what it once was, though I still remember him, sitting across the room and hating. Yes, I remember that." She smiled blissfully up at me.

"Hyannis killed his wife. Pushed her in front of a car, poor thing. Of course, all the others said he hadn't. Swore she'd tripped and fell. Profaned themselves before God and bought eternal fire. The judge acquitted him, though the other girl told the truth." She shook her head. "Texas. I remember it all so clearly."

"Texas." I leaned forward, watching her old, faded eyes. "What was his name, do you remember?"

"His name?" Her face screwed up a little at that. "Such a *long* time ago, when one's memory is frail. Daniel?" She tipped her head, frowning in consideration.

"Daniel?" She wondered again, face clouded. "No." The cloud cleared; she raised a triumphant forefinger. "*David.* All the way down in Austin, Texas. My, yes. David. Pretty David Foxwell."

## 22

I DROVE HOME.

I know I drove home, because the Camaro was in the barn, later. But I couldn't have told you anything about the drive, except that very likely it was done too fast.

The next thing I do remember is pushing open the ell door and walking into the kitchen, slinging jacket and pocketbook onto the table. The message light was blinking on the answering machine. I pushed the replay.

"Jen, it's Merry. I'm at Harry's house. I'm going to be staying here a couple days— at least until the rest of the sheep're rounded up. Heather and Jim Pickett found four or five of them over by their place and got them behind fence; the rest are kind of trickling in— " a soft exhalation here, maybe a laugh.

"Harry says come on over for supper— you're too damn' thin." There was a pause. "Call me, okay? Even if you can't do supper. I'd like to— I'd like to say thanks." She cleared her throat. "Talk to you soon." There was a faint fizz of line noise, then the sharp click of a receiver being set down.

I ran the tape back and reset the machine. Then I brewed some coffee and carried the mug upstairs to my room.

\*\*\*

THE NET IS NOT JUST a motley collection of shops, speakeasies, and electronic message centers. It does offer weightier fare.

For those of a studious turn of mind, there's Online University, with its schedule of interactive and home-study

courses. Net users can study anything from creative writing
to nuclear physics at Online U. OU did not currently give
a degree, but Net gossip hinted of a deal in the works with
a prestigious non-virtual school.

For those with a burning need to know... almost
anything... there is the Library.

Library access is not a standard Net option. It costs
extra— a lot extra— and is granted on a case-by-case basis
by an on-line monitor.

ID? the Librarian barked.

JENNIFER A. PIERCE, WIMSY, MAINE, I
typed, and added my Net account code.

REASON FOR ACCESS REQUEST?

I'M A REPORTER, COVERING LOCAL
SUSPICIOUS DEATH. I NEED BACKGROUND
INFO.

I got the impression of a "hmmph" before the
Librarian demanded, SEARCH STRING.

In my room, I rubbed cold hands together, then
flexed my fingers and typed: ABORTION PROTESTS,
DEATHS RELATED, AREA AUSTIN TEXAS,
KEYWORDS: REVEREND STERN, HYANNIS
STERN, FOXWELL, DAVID FOXWELL, MAINE.

TIMEFRAME? The Librarian snapped.

FIVE YEARS TO PRESENT.

THAT SEARCH WILL TAKE SEVERAL
MINUTES, the Librarian warned.

MY CREDIT'S GOOD.

I SEE THAT, the Librarian said peevishly.
PREPARE TO ACCEPT DOWNLOAD. YOU WILL
NOT BE TOLD AGAIN. SEARCH STRING
INITIATED.

The screen went blank.

I set up the download file, opened and triggered it,

then sat stiffly back in my chair, sipping cold coffee and staring at the blank blue screen, telling myself hopeful lies.

*It's all going to come to smoke,* I told myself. *She's a crazy lady. A very crazy lady. And even if it is David Foxwell— even if it's a true memory and not a crazy-dream— that still doesn't have to mean it's Fox.*

Fox, who believed in ghosts. Who hated, oh my yes, and who had only recently fulfilled a vow.

The computer bleeped raucously. On the screen a graph flicked into being, displaying the size of the file being transmitted and estimating a time to completion.

The graph changed, now showing how much data had been received; how much there was yet to receive.

Thirty percent. Fifty. Sixty-five. Eighty. Ninety-five. "Beeeep!"

DOWNLOAD COMPLETE

I reached to the keyboard, closed the file, coded in the log-off and tumbled out of the Net, back to reality.

Reality was ice-cold hands and a curious tightness in my chest. I ignored both, and initiated the program that would open my research.

\*\*\*

THE DATA PACKET contained mostly news clippings, covering a period of many months. The story was muddled here and there by frequent retelling, but the plot went like this:

It had happened thirty-three months ago. In Austin, Texas.

Reverend Hyannis Stern of Wimsy, Maine, abortionist hunter extraordinaire, had traveled to Austin and organized local like-minded people to form a human barricade around a downtown abortion clinic, refusing, at first, to let anyone inside.

Clinic workers called the cops. The cops issued orders: Reverend Stern and his buddies could exercise their right of protest, but they could not physically prevent anyone from entering or leaving the clinic. They posted one— count him— one— cop to enforce this edict.

So ordered, Reverend Stern and his friends— law-abiding citizens, all— took up their signs, their songs and their slogans. They allowed clinic personnel to report for work— through a storm of catcalls and hard names.

Day after day, they lined up by the door to the clinic, posters at the ready, and alternately pled with, cajoled, prayed for, and scorned any client who approached the clinic. Most of those, seeing the intensity and the number in the crowd they would have to pass through, simply turned and ran. At least one girl threw hysterics right there on the sidewalk in front of the place, a circumstance that moved Butchie to deliver one of the finest extemporaneous sermons of his career.

The siege went on. And a resistance movement solidified.

Volunteers of both genders signed up as escorts, sworn to help clinic patients safely through Butchie's gauntlet of fury.

One of those volunteers was a woman named Kathy Foxwell.

The computer file did not include a picture of Kathy Foxwell— wire photos tend to break up badly when scanned. The narrative described her as petite, a librarian by trade. She had not been a member of the local Pro-Choice group. By all accounts she had not been one of Butchie's arch-enemies, a "militant feminist."

She had been, as so many of the volunteers had been,

simply a person who perceived an injustice, and was moved to do her best to right it.

In spite of her size— or perhaps because of it—Kathy was a remarkably successful escort. Three times, she traversed the line, a frightened girl or woman tucked under her tiny wing.

The fourth time, she died.

Reports of the incident varied significantly. The girl Kathy had been escorting— one Sarajane Hebert— swore under oath in a court of law that "the tall man in the suit— yessir, him there" had lunged out of the crowd toward her, that Kathy had put herself between Sarajane and the tall man. That the tall man had pushed Kathy— "hard, sir— he meant to hurt her"— off the sidewalk and into the path of an oncoming car.

Butchie's adherents said otherwise: that Kathy had tripped and fallen; that Butchie had tried to pull her back from the edge of the curb.

The cop had been on the far side of the crowd, unaware of disaster until the scream and the thump and the wail of abused brakes jerked him forward— too late.

Kathy Foxwell, 29 years old, petite and gutsy, was dead, leaving behind her husband of five years, David, a computer programmer.

The driver of the car, an elderly tourist from Minnesota, was not charged. He had been driving within— indeed, somewhat below— the posted limit. Kathy had fallen directly beneath his wheels.

Hyannis Stern was charged with murder, and in his case the machineries of law had moved startlingly fast. The trial lasted a scant four days. The jury appeared to have entirely discounted testimony from Sarajane— sixteen, pregnant and clearly unlettered—- preferring to believe in the fundamental honesty of gentlemen and ladies who wear nice clothes and speak in soft voices.

Butchie was victoriously acquitted. The clinic shut down. In Austin, things settled, shifted— slept.

Two years and nine months further down the timeline, in a cool attic room in Wimsy, Maine, I rubbed cold hands over my hot face, and noticed, distantly, that I was shaking.

After a while, I looked back at the screen. There was one file left to read.

It was a bio, clipped from the tongue-in-cheek hyper-mag, *Cyberspace Review.*

"Foxwell, David Edward. DOB 07/31/58, Osaka, Japan, m. 1986 Kathleen Marie Jackson, deceased. Game designer, strategy/simulation. Trademark awesome graphics; complex, brain-twisting plots; gut-wrenching realism and genuine wit. Lord Fox of Cyberspace, by order and acknowledgment of the Council of Virtual Knights."

I closed my eyes. Fox. It *was* Fox.

\*\*\*

THERE WAS NO DAVID Foxwell listed in the local phone book. There was no David Foxwell listed with the operator. Nor was there an Edward Foxwell or any other combination that came handily to mind. Random Access was listed as a new account, data line only. The operator was sorry not to be able to give me the street address.

I dialed Random Access, ran for the main menu and punched <P>.

*Calling Fox. One Moment Please.*

It was much longer than a moment. I sat hunched forward in my chair, hands fisted on the arms.

"Fox. Come *on*, Fox. Answer the page."

*I'm sorry,* Random Access told me. *Fox can't come to the computer right now. Please feel free to leave him e-mail.*

I swallowed hard in a dust-dry throat. Hit <P> again.

*The sysop is not available for chat,* Random Access told me sternly. *You may leave private e-mail or post a message in The Speakeasy.*

For maybe five seconds I sat there, my finger poised over <P>, my breath coming in ragged gasps, as if I was crying. I moved my finger, touched <G> for Goodbye, and logged off.

***

HOW DO YOU FIND A man who doesn't want to be found?

There are ways, of course. Given time, patience and a certain number of committed searchers, even the wiliest fox can be run to earth. David Foxwell had to eat, after all. He very likely owned a car. Certainly, he had a phone.

A cop could shake the location of that data phone out of an operator in two seconds flat and not even be breathing hard at the end of it. Cops had access to Department of Motor Vehicle records. Given time, cops had access to the records of every department of motor vehicles from Wimsy to San Ysidro.

"It's a cop thing, Jen," I told myself, sitting with eyes closed in the cold cocoon of my room.

But I didn't want to call the cops.

See, the thing I love about computer bulletin boards— the thing that keeps drawing me back to the nets— is that the people I meet there are *honest.* They're not, of course:

cyberpeople are just as venal as flesh-and-bone people. But in cyberspace, where no one knows you— whether you're in a wheelchair, or deaf; whether you're an attorney, an actor or an art thief— there's very little reason to lie the lies we lie in the flesh.

On the nets, bodies left behind with chair, Mercedes, and the daily, dreary rat-race, people are only themselves: pure thought, free to express and experience.

For someone with a basic distrust of human people, a yearning to *know about* human people, and an overly vivid imagination, cyberspace is Disneyland, the Nautilus and Never-never-land, all tied up in one mouth-watering package.

Imagine a whole universe, full of imaginary friends.

My imagination provided voices for my friends on the nets; it provided an assumption of basic decency and goodwill on the part of everyone I met there.

And I trusted the person I imagined Fox to be.

"Jennifer, Fox has very likely killed a man, and he is now just as likely letting someone else take the heat for it." I fisted my hands on the chair arms and tensed my arms, straining against my own inertia. "It's for the cops, Jennifer. Call them."

But I sat there, one minute, two minutes, longer, thinking how very easy it is, really— without a face— to lie.

\*\*\*

I WENT DOWN THE STAIRS in the dark, flicked on the kitchen light and started across to lock the door.

Too late.

From four feet away, I watched the door swing slowly open, groaning on its ancient hinges. I froze, and thought of one more thing: Fox had my address. I'd given it to him when I signed on to his board.

The door swung wider and I watched, mesmerized, heartbeat pounding in my ears.

Finally, its swing was stopped by the wall and he stepped in, the light gleaming gold along his hair. He was smiling. There was a gun in his right hand.

"Hi, Jenny," he said, and the smile became a grin. "Home all alone?"

# 23

"GET THE HELL OUT of here." My voice was firm, I heard with astonishment, even— angry.

Craig's eyes opened wide; he glanced drolly down at the gun, then back at me, eyebrows raised.

"I don't think so," he said, and came another step inside.

I went back a step in response; froze as the gun came up.

"Good girl," he said, and pointed. "Sit down."

I pulled the chair out from beneath the table and sat on the edge, forcing myself to watch his face, not the gun.

"Relax," he said, reaching out and grabbing the edge of the door. One-handed, he swung it shut. It hit the frame with a noise like a shot and I jumped. Craig laughed.

"So," he said conversationally. "Where's the other bitch?"

"Which," I asked, and my voice was not so steady, now, "other bitch?"

"Miss Bo-Peep, no barn, no sheep. Burned some good, didn't it?" He laughed again; sobered like a switch being flicked. "I been to the other house— place is empty. I figured she must've come here, since you and her are such good friends."

Carefully, I shook my head. "Bad guess."

"Yeah?" He looked at me consideringly, head tipped a little to one side. "You know what, though, Jenny? I don't believe you." The gun moved. "Call her."

I blinked. "Call her?" I repeated stupidly and Craig frowned.

"Yeah, call her. You know, 'Merry, come down

here.' Like that." In peripheral vision, the gun moved again. I kept my eyes on his face and licked my lips.

"Merry!" I sang out. "Can you help me with this, please?"

Silence in the house and all around.

"Again," Craig ordered.

"Hey, Merry! I need some help here!" All too true. My heart was pounding heavily; the surface of my skin was quivery, all over goose bumps.

Nothing. I let the silence grow for a beat for five, then said, in a voice that cracked and trembled.

"I told you she wasn't here."

The phone rang.

*Oh, God,* I thought. *Please don't let it be her, calling me back...*

On the fourth ring, the answering machine picked up. The tape fizzed for a second, then my voice came in, sounding professionally perky.

"Hi, this is Jennifer Pierce. I can't come to the phone right now, but if you'll leave your name, number and a brief message, I'll be glad to call you back. Wait for the beep."

The beep came. The person on the other end of the line cleared their throat.

"Jennifer, this is Marian Younger." Relief washed through me like a physical pain. I bit my lip and kept my eyes on Craig's face, on which there was no expression at all.

"I thought you might want to come over and take a look at my new modem," Marian was saying. "It's a fifty-eight-six internal and I just finished installing it...." The painfully young voice faded out; I heard the police scanner shriek and garble in the background. "Well, if you're not home... I'll talk to you later. You don't have to call me back."

There was some rattling noise, as if Marian was having

trouble reseating the receiver, then the click of the line being disconnected.

My heart was going to bust right out of my chest if it beat any harder. I tried to swallow, but my throat didn't seem to be working too well.

Before me, Craig— the man with the gun—shook his head sadly. "Well, now. What am I going to do with you?"

I tried to swallow again. "Why do you have to do anything with me?" I asked huskily.

"Now, Jenny, don't play stupid. You're real smart, I know that. Just like I know she told you everything— Merry did." Again, the sorrowful headshake.

"Now, *that* was dumb, telling me that she knew all about it like that— *threatening* me. There's ways she could've handled it, if she wanted her old man off the hook. She could've talked to somebody higher up—worked a deal, maybe. But she wanted to throw her weight around." He sighed. "Doesn't work that way. I got my job. I got my standing orders. No mess. No loose ends." He smiled, looking like Everywoman's dream lover.

"That's you," he said softly. "A loose end."

"I'm not a loose end if Merry didn't tell me anything," I said and took a deep breath. "Craig, look. Just put the gun away and get the hell out, okay?"

He shook his head. "Sending a cop around to see me— you think I'm scared of these hick cops, Jenny?" He laughed. "Stupid fucker. Wanted to see my ID. I showed him ID. Sure I did." He tipped his head, staring at me with ocean-blue eyes.

"Went to see Old Lady Stern today, didn't you? She tell you how her old man blew all her money? She tell you how he played the horses— how he borrowed heavy and owed lots of bread down south?" Another sad shake of the gold-crowned head. "Smart girl, Jenny. Too damn smart to live."

I stared at him while my brain helpfully replayed part of my interview with Colin Wyandotte: "There'll be no monkeying with the odds or any other cunning trick like they might play down Rhode Island...." and then another snippet, this one played against the bang, clatter and clash of the Division: "See where ol' Righteous won't be playing the ponies much as he used to...."

"You work for the Mafia?" I asked stupidly.

He shrugged. "Hey, it's a job. I'm good at it. This one should've gone down easy. Bad luck the ambulance tech took his job so serious. Bad luck Merry's old man been Special Forces." He shrugged again. "You can't get all the breaks, you know? And now there's loose ends. My boss don't like loose ends." He sighed.

"What I think, Jenny, is you and me ought to go for a ride."

"A ride."

"Yeah, I think that's how it'll go down. Everybody in town knows how fast you drive. Nobody's going to be real surprised to find you wrapped around a tree." He smiled. "Besides, you said car crashes run in your family." The gun moved.

"Let's go."

\*\*\*

I SLID INTO THE driver's seat, closed the door; automatically pulled the seatbelt tight. Craig got in the other side, reached over, slid the key into the ignition and turned it. The engine caught immediately, purring hungrily to life. Numbly, I brought up the lights.

"Okay, Jenny," Craig settled sideways in the bucket seat, facing me. The gun gleamed in the light from the dash. "Don't try anything funny from the movies. Just drive the car and do like I tell you. Be a good girl and I'll make it so it won't hurt too much. Okay?"

And they said chivalry was dead.

"Okay," I whispered and put the car into gear.

I backed out of the barn, straightened her up and rolled round the corner, through the dooryard and up the drive. The Camaro was purring like a tiger.

Beside me, Craig watched, one shoulder braced against the door. Not belted in, of course. Real men don't fasten their seat belts. Not even when they're sitting in what my uncle the state cop calls "the deadman's seat."

At the top of the drive, I stopped.

"What's right?" Craig asked.

"The river."

"Go left."

I went left, obeying the twenty-five-mile-per-hour limit for possibly the first time in my life.

Wimsy is not a town to waste good money lighting up the puckerbrush. The Point Road was darker than the inside of a monk's hood. I brought up the high beams, dazzling a deer at the road's edge. I touched the brakes; the deer leapt into the road. A second leap carried her into the trees at the other side.

"What the hell are you stopping for?" Craig demanded.

"You want me to hit a deer?" I snapped back.

There was a moment's silence.

"Nah," he said. "Wouldn't be enough, at this speed."

It would have been enough for both of us, if the deer had leapt into the windshield, as a woman from Massachusetts had discovered last year, over to China. I didn't bother sharing that anecdote with Craig.

Near the top of the Point Road, he said, "Hold it."

I touched the brake, heart in mouth, hands like ice on the leather-covered wheel.

"Nah," Craig said, real soft. "No sense making it complicated." He nodded at me. "Okay, Jenny. Go on up to the corner and take a right."

I eased past the Ash's driveway, went to the end of the road and took a right.

He had me turn left at the intersection with the Stone Road and I suddenly knew where this was going to end.

"What'm I supposed to be doing down at the quarry this time of night?" I asked, and was surprised to find my voice almost conversational.

Craig shrugged. "I don't know, Jenny. Maybe you meet your girlfriend there, huh? Or maybe you just felt like seeing how good this baby hugs the road, and lost it on the last curve like that kid, couple weeks ago."

"Yeah," I breathed, which was about all I could manage, with my chest tight as it was. I was going to end up at the bottom of the quarry, sticky blood pudding coating rocks and the sharded metal of what had once been a car. And Merry was going to wind up there, too— or someplace else just as permanent.

Beside me, Craig reached up, pushing roughly at the catch for the sunroof.

"Be careful! That comes off," I snapped, like he was a roughneck kid instead of a very scary man holding a gun.

Craig laughed, yanked the catch and straightened his arm with a shove. I heard the crack as the snap-hinge gave; saw the Plexiglas sheet tumble away in a corner of the rear-view mirror.

"Bastard," I said and Craig laughed again, settling back

into his corner.

"Pretty night," he observed. "Pick it up a little, Jenny. I want to see your hair blowing in the breeze."

My heart stopped. My lungs locked. My brain went dead. From within an icy internal silence, I turned my head and stared at him.

He smiled, moved the gun. "Open up a couple buttons. I want to see what I'm going to be getting into." The smile went away. "Do it."

I did it, fingers fumbling on the slick plastic. Somewhere during that exercise my brain came back on-line, coolly running a checklist.

*Driver belted?*

Check.

*Passenger unbelted?*

Check.

*Forward velocity sufficient?*

I eased down on the gas, belatedly obeying Craig's other instruction. The wind of our passage ran skeleton fingers into my hair, lifting it away from my face. I glanced at the speedometer: thirty-five miles per hour.

Check.

The landscape through which the Stone Road passes is lunar in nature. Boulders cluster in vari-sized groups, throwing weird shadows on the scant meadow grass beneath the influence of the high half-moon. The nearer one gets to the quarry, the more numerous the rocks become, shouldering each other up out of the meadow, to lower and loom at the verge of the road.

The high-beams picked up the edge of a big one on the right, seemingly perched on the road itself. I glanced at Craig, his back against the door, the gun alert in his hand. The breeze from the hole in the roof ruffled his hair. He intercepted my glance and smiled.

I brought my eyes back to the road. On my right, the big rock loomed. Mica glittered along its surface, wakened by the caress of the headlights. The speedometer showed steady at thirty-eight miles per hour.

I twisted the wheel to the right.

\*\*\*

I DON'T REMEMBER actually hitting the boulder. Maybe I blacked out for a couple seconds. Or maybe terror wiped the memory, like a computer wiping an unneeded file.

The next thing I do remember is thinking the engine sounded wrong, and reaching out blind to turn the key. I seemed to be at a very peculiar angle, too— listing hard to the right, though the belt held me tight— too tight— to the driver's seat.

I opened my eyes, looking out through the shattered windshield at a landscape of rock, gray and black in the light of the waning moon.

Cautiously, I turned my head, looking down at the passenger's door, where Craig was sprawled.

Heart pounding, I reached to the instrument panel and spun on the inside lights.

There was blood in the golden hair. Blood masked the left side of the scraped and battered face. His right arm was twisted at a bad angle. From my vantage point, it didn't look like he was breathing.

I sagged against the straps, almost sobbing in relief, and sent up a brief prayer of thanksgiving to whatever god or goddess might have duty this evening.

Dead. Dead and done.

Which left only the tidy problem of how I was going to get out of here.

Clumsily, disoriented by the angle, I got a grip on the door latch, and worked it.

Nothing happened.

I swallowed against panic and tried again.

Nothing.

I closed my eyes, forcibly quelling panic. *Take it easy, Jennifer. This is not Death Valley. A car hitting a stone wall makes a lot of noise. Somebody will be along, sooner or later.*

Sure.

I opened my eyes and looked up, through the hole in the roof, seeing nothing but an army of boulders, marching away to the black treeline.

The Galen farm was half-a-mile or so away. They might well have heard the noise and were even now mounting a scouting party.

And if they were, I decided, there wasn't any harm in hurrying them along.

I hit the horn.

A hand snatched out of nowhere, grabbing my wrist with brutal force and yanking me back. I gasped, too terrified to scream.

"Stupid bitch," Craig snarled, twisting my wrist hard. I shrank back against the seat, and all I could think was that I was trapped, trapped— and the only thing I'd done was to make it easy for him....

"I'm going to kill you, Jenny. And this time I'll make sure it hurts." He shook my wrist, fingers cutting into flesh.

I blinked at him, stupid with terror. Blood was running hard from beneath the matted hair. The left side of his face was sheeted; blood dripped off his chin and onto his shirt.

Abruptly, he released me, and raised his hand to

wipe at the blood-fouled eye. A breeze came up, danced through the hole in the roof and departed. Craig looked up. When he looked back to me, he was smiling.

"Ever see a car fire?" he asked, conversationally. "They go up real fast. Anybody trapped inside just— bakes alive." He eased back, shifting his position, glanced up at the hole again and nodded.

"You wait right here," he told me, and straightened, boots against the inside of the passenger's door.

He put his left arm through the hole, then his head. I watched, mesmerized, and barely took note of the first, very slight, rocking.

Craig twisted, got his bad arm and his shoulders into the space. Around me, the Camaro shifted, and I heard metal scraping rock, down below the passenger's door.

Beside me, Craig paused in his labors. I heard his fingers scrabbling along the roof, searching out a hold.

The Camaro rocked.

Craig gathered himself and suddenly pushed outward, through the hole, disturbing the car's precarious center of balance. He twisted, and was very nearly halfway out when the Camaro rocked once more, heavily, to the right.

And crashed flat onto its roof.

# 24

SO MY DAD WAS RIGHT, after all, and I wound up being cut out of a wreck.

Then Wimsy Rescue gave me a ride over to Waterville, where the emergency room doctor fussed over my bruises, drew a vial of blood and asked me three times if I knew how goddamned lucky I was that the goddamned seat belts had held.

I asked him if he thought hanging upside down for two hours while a couple of volunteer firemen used a giant can opener on your car was a picnic, and he told me I might have a mild concussion.

"It can only improve things," I said, and he snorted.

"Real attitude case, aren't you?"

"A lifelong affliction." I sat up on the gurney, which all my bruises insisted was a mistake, but I was damned if I was going to lie back down now that I was up. "Am I dismissed?"

He sighed. "Hang around 'til I get the stuff back from X-ray, okay? You notice anything funny— fuzzy vision, sudden pain in your head or eyes, tell the nurse. We'll get a chair and wheel you out to the lounge."

"I'd rather walk," I told him.

"I know."

\*\*\*

THE AIDE WHEELED ME down the hall to the deserted lounge.

"There's a nurse's station right outside the door,"

she told me, like I hadn't seen it when we'd wheeled past. "If you start to feel bad, you just holler and she'll be right over, okay?"

I felt plenty bad already, but I didn't think she'd be interested, so I nodded as much as my wrenched neck would allow and said, "Okay."

She smiled and patted my hand and bustled importantly away.

I closed my eyes and tried very hard not to think, in which enterprise I was but marginally successful.

My brain *would* keep reviewing the calculations that had led to my deliberate run at the rock. The impact should have been enough to kill my passenger: there was no use pretending I hadn't meant to kill him, like there was no use pretending he hadn't deserved killing.

But it bothered me that the crash itself hadn't accounted for Craig. I remembered my uncle the state cop's dissertation on the subject very plainly— *thirty-five miles an hour, you're belted and your passenger isn't— the surest way is to hit a tree. Impact will kill the passenger, nine times out of ten. You've got some bruises, maybe some bones broken—but you're alive. And that's the point.*

That's the point.

My brain finally got tired of re-running its calculations and I sat there in the wheelchair, eyes closed against the fluorescent glare, blessedly without thought.

From the nurse's hall station came the muted clatter of keys, and her voice, muted also, holding brief one-way conversations.

Maybe I dozed.

The sound of my own name roused me.

"...Pierce?" A man's voice, light and very clear. Not a voice I recognized.

The nurse murmured; the man answered.

"David Foxwell. I— "

"Fox." The first try came out as a hoarse whisper. I tried again.

"Fox!"

He heard. I saw shadows shift in the hallway, then he came into the lounge, not hurrying, not dallying, and stood before me, hands in the pockets of his beat-up leather jacket.

He was one of those honey-skinned redheads; a shade too thin; nose too long; chin definitely pointed. His eyes were an extraordinary cobalt blue— almost black— surrounded by thick auburn lashes.

"Oh, but how those eyes could *hate*!" Jackie Stern's voice giggled in my back brain.

Right now, the eyes were concerned.

"Jennifer," he said, and it wasn't a question. "What happened?"

I swallowed. "Wrecked my car." I took a shaky breath. "Why are you here?"

One side of the firm mouth lifted— maybe a smile. "Marian. I got home and the sysop page was going off like the Fourth of July at the Alamo. She didn't let me type a word, just started yelling that you were here and that you needed me." He tipped his head, thin brows pulling together. "Do you need me?"

"Yes." I said and it felt like the truest word I'd ever spoken.

"All right," he said and glanced around. "What are you doing now?"

"Waiting for the X-rays." I swallowed, abruptly knowing what else I was waiting for. "And for the cops."

Fox nodded, shucked the jacket and tossed it across the back of the chair next to me before sitting there himself. He was wearing old jeans, old boots, and a flannel shirt so worn it showed nap like velvet. A pair of gold-rimmed glasses rode loose in the breast pocket. His hands were long-fingered. Ringless.

I looked at him and shook my head, which woke a million protesting neck muscles.

He raised an eyebrow.

"Osaka, Japan?" I asked.

"Air Force." He lifted a hand, ticking geographies off on long, lazy fingers. "Also Germany, Italy, England, Hawaii— " He inclined his head, mouth curving faintly upward. "And Texas."

I felt my own mouth move toward a smile. "Of course. What could be more natural?"

"Almost anything," Fox said seriously. "But the natives seem fond of it."

In the midst of becoming a laugh, the sound twisted. I gasped and tears started, blurring Fox into a tangle of auburn and honey.

"Jennifer?"

I gasped again, bit my lip, managed to blink back the tears, to push back the instant when I knew the car was going to go over the rest of the way— and got him clear in my sight.

"There's someone dead," I said, voice wobbling bad. "In the wreck. I killed him."

Pity flashed through those extraordinary eyes. He leaned forward, holding out a hand. "It was an accident, Jennifer."

"No," I said breathlessly. "No, I meant to— "

Shadows moved; the lights came up abruptly and it was Bruce Gagnon coming across the lounge, John Therriault at his side.

***

THEY PULLED A COUPLE chairs close and got themselves situated, notebooks at the ready. John looked up with his easy smile.

"Jenny. How're you feeling?"

I looked at him; decided that he really wanted to know. "Like I kissed a rock and rolled my car. The doctor's trying to sell me a concussion. He wants to look at the X-rays before he lets me go home, but nothing seems broken." I wrinkled my nose. "Just all over bruised."

He nodded. "I'd stay away from that concussion," he said, flipping open the notebook. "What I hear, the doc's overpriced."

"They're cheaper in Freeport," I agreed, and John smiled again before letting his eyes move to Fox.

"He's a friend," I said. John clicked his pen.

"Name," he didn't ask Fox.

"David Foxwell."

John wrote. "Address."

"I'm renting the carriage house on the Currier estate, off the Winding Road."

Simple as that. John made his note, then glanced up.

"We're going to be asking Jenny a couple questions, Mr. Foxwell. If you'd like to wait down the hall, we'll let you know when we're through."

Fox lifted an eyebrow, but otherwise stayed precisely put.

Across from me, Bruce Gagnon sighed. "Are you a lawyer, Mr. Foxwell?"

"I'm a friend, Jennifer said." Fox considered Bruce for a moment out of bland cobalt eyes, then turned to me.

"Your lawyer should be here for this. These gentleman can wait while you make the call."

"I don't have a lawyer," I told him and looked to John. "Craig burned down the Ash's barn, and he was going to kill me. I ran into the rock deliberately."

John nodded, easy-going as always. "Crash kill him?"

I remembered not to shake my head. "No. He tried to climb out the sunroof and the— the car fell on top of him." I swallowed forcibly— this was no time to develop a queasy stomach.

John nodded again and made a note in his book. He glanced up, looking serious and friendly. "Want to tell me about it?"

No, I didn't. And Fox was right: I should make them wait while I somehow rustled up a lawyer. The effort of that loomed gargantuan. I wanted to go home. I wanted to lock the door and scream until I was hoarse, which, considering the state of my throat, would be all of thirty seconds.

I took a deep breath and met John's eyes.

"Sure," I said.

\*\*\*

IT DIDN'T MAKE EASY telling, but I told it as straight as I knew how, from the time Craig walked into the kitchen to the moment I knew the Camaro was going to finish its roll. Around the almost-stop at the Ash's farm, I started shaking pretty bad— adrenaline. Fox put his hand out, no comment, and I held on for dear life while I told the telling down.

At the end of it, I stopped, gulping for air, and looked from Bruce to John.

"That's it," I said. "Do your worst."

Bruce glowered, but John smiled and shook his head.

"I went around to talk with the boy like I said I would, Jenny. Ran the ID. Got a phone call back on it late today. Turns out Rhode Island State troopers are real interested in that license number. Real interested in talking with Craig Thomas Henderson. Asked if I might point him out, should one of their fellas make the drive up." He nodded. "Found the gun. Might be Rhode Island's interested in that, too." He glanced at Bruce.

"Sheriff?"

"I question the connection with the murder investigation," Bruce said slowly. "The Reverend played the ponies wicked— whole town knew that. But the story that he owed gambling debts to the Mafia—"

"Is very likely true," Fox said placidly.

Both cops turned to stare at him.

"You were acquainted with Craig Henderson, Mr. Foxwell?" That was Bruce.

Fox shook his head. "No. But I have an— extensive— file on Hyannis Stern. My lawyer can bring it to you tomorrow, if you think it will move Scott Ash's release along more speedily."

Bruce looked a little dazed. "It might," he allowed. "Tell your lawyer I'll be glad to see him."

"Certainly."

John flipped his book closed.

"All right, Jenny, here's what we're going to do. I'm going to write you up for reckless driving— "

"Reckless driving?" I demanded. "There wasn't anything reckless about my driving!"

"Reckless driving," John repeated firmly, and Fox squeezed my hand. I subsided, though not without a certain feeling of ill-use.

"Might need to talk with you again," John continued. "Straighten out a few points. I'll call and let you know what we find out on that gun. In the meantime— " a glance at Bruce, who nodded. "In the meantime, I think your friend can take you hom He stood.

"Goodnight."

Bruce was up, too, and turning to go. He turned back. "S for you," he said, "out at the front desk. From the car." He was gone before I could muster a thanks, John on his heels.

They were immediately succeeded by a perky little brune wearing a nurse's uniform, though I swear she looked no older tl twelve. She was, however, the bearer of joyful news.

"Ms. Pierce? Doctor Norris says you can go home— the X rays are fine. If the bruises bother you, you can take up to three aspirin every four hours."

"Terrific." I stood up quick, before she hatched the notion of wheeling me down the hall, ignored the roaring in my ears and the stars spangling across my vision. Fox was up, too, pulling on jacket.

"Let's go," I said.

# 25

WE STOPPED AT THE desk and I claimed my stuff— junk from the glove compartment, all jumbled together in a plastic bag, and the old umbrella I'd kept in the trunk.

"Hold it," said the receptionist. "You don't want to forget this." She ducked under the desk and came up with a roll of winterizing plastic in her arms, looking pleased as punch.

I stared at it, fighting an almost overpowering desire to laugh. *If I start now, I'm not going to be able to stop...*

A hand landed lightly on my shoulder. "Steady," Fox murmured in my ear, and leaned forward to take the roll from the girl.

"Thank you," he said gravely and she dimpled. He looked back at me. "Ready, Jennifer?"

I managed one nearly calm breath— then another, licked my lips and nodded.

"Ready."

We went down the hall together, through the automatic doors and into the vapor-lit night.

An emerald green four-by-four was the only vehicle in the visitor's lot. Fox led me to it, opened the passenger's door. I got myself into the leather bucket seat, swearing silently. Meanwhile, Fox opened the back door and stowed the plastic, the umbrella and the junk.

I snapped down the seatbelt, wincing as the webbing tightened over the bruises from the Camaro's belts. Fox swung behind the wheel, slid the key home and turned it. The CD player kicked in the instant the truck purred awake: I heard three chords from Mark Knopfler's guitar before Fox touched the switch and cut it off. He locked his belt into place and glanced over to me.

"I'll need directions."

"Right." I raised my arm to point, and every muscle from the fingertip to the back of my neck screamed bloody murder. "Go thou to Wimsy and pick up Preble Street, follow it to the Mill Road, thence to the Stone Road. Go left on the Stone Road— "

Abruptly, I closed my eyes. The adrenal rush was less intense this time, leaving me covered in goose-bumps.

"Is there," Fox was asking calmly, "another way home?"

My head was resting against the back of the high leather seat. I didn't bother to lift it, just rolled in back and forth in negation. "Richmond's Ferry stopped running twenty years ago," I said, and my voice sounded thin in my own ears. "It's the last house on the Point."

"All right. Is there somewhere else you can go tonight? Today."

"I've got to feed my cat," I said, and rolled my head to look at him. His mouth tightened and I half-raised a hand. It was too heavy to lift all the way.

"I promise not to lose it, Fox, okay?"

For a second, I thought he was going to give me an argument. Then he nodded and put the truck into gear.

I sagged into the leather bucket seat, closed my eyes, and let myself ache horribly for a beat of twelve. Then I pried my eyes open again; found Fox watching me.

"You can sleep if you want," he said, looking back to the road. "I assume I turn left on the Point Road and keep on going until I find the river?"

"Nope," I said, and delivered the Maine-ism absently.

"You hit the river, you gone too fah. I'm the last mailbox on the right."

"Across the road from where the church used to be?" he asked, deadpan.

I felt my mouth form a smile. "You've been there?"

It was impossible to tell in the meager light from the dash, but I thought he smiled when he looked back to me. "Get some rest."

I sighed and closed my eyes once more, letting the leather cuddle me. The truck's ride was silky: I felt a slight ripple when we passed over the Division's track at the bridge, and stirred.

"Fox?"

"Yes."

"I went to see Mrs. Stern today— yesterday," I said, eyes still closed. "She'd been waiting almost three years for you to kill her husband."

Silence. The truck continued its smooth progress— no faster, no slower, than previously.

"I suppose she'll have to learn to live with diminished expectations," he said eventually.

I sighed. "After I saw her," I said, "I went home and called the Library. Pulled the files about— " I hesitated.

"About Kathy," Fox said emotionlessly. "I can bear to hear her name, thank you."

"All right," I said and sighed again. "In a nutshell, I was convinced. I had your word that you hadn't been at the barn-raising— but people lie. I didn't— don't— know that you have the special training that was necessary. But you had a damn good reason to want him dead— and you're here, in Butchie's own home town. All the way from Texas."

There was a short silence. The truck made the turn onto Main Street.

"Did you call the police?" Fox asked quietly.

I opened my eyes, watching his profile as he watched the road.

"No. I didn't call the police. I told myself to call the police, but I didn't. I called the board. You didn't answer the page."

He glanced over, eyes black in the meager light. "What time?"

"Around eight. Maybe eight-thirty."

He nodded. "I'd gone to meet a friend for a beer." Another glance. "Bill Jacques, as it happens." Quiet for the beat of three. He took the left onto Preble Street.

"What were you going to do, Jennifer? Ask me to give myself up?"

"I'm not sure," I confessed. "See, I— I trusted you. I didn't want it to be you, but if it had— if you'd killed Butchie— I could understand it. Not condone it, but understand it. What I couldn't understand was why you were letting someone else take the heat. It— didn't seem like you. You didn't know Scott. He hadn't hurt you— or yours. So, yeah. I might have asked you that— to give yourself up and let Scott have his life."

He flicked a look to me. "That would have been remarkably dangerous, don't you think?"

"Oh, I was scared," I admitted. "But I didn't want it to be you, Fox."

"Things are," he said sternly, "whether you want them to be or not."

"I know," I said. "I do know that."

There was a moment of silence. "Sorry," he said, and I heard him sigh. "Jennifer, it very well could have been me. I had it all planned— I can show you the gun, if you like." He slowed; made the turn from Preble onto Mill.

"Fortunately, it occurred to me in time that I am not

only a rotten shot, but that shooting people is illegal." He glanced over. "It upset Kathy when I did things that were illegal."

I blinked. "Did you do a lot of illegal things?"

"A few, now and then— fewer, after a while. Marriage was a mitigating influence. At any rate, it also occurred to me that while I'm not a good shot, I am a very, very good computer geek, and that there are more ways to kill a man than by simply putting a bullet through his head."

"So you started to build a file."

"I started to build a file," Fox agreed. "I uncovered the gambling early on, but I wanted particulars— facts: names, places, amounts. I wanted to crucify him, to totally discredit him, with his family, with his town and with his cause. That sort of detail takes a little longer. And when I thought I had it all— or at least enough— I found another thread."

"The Mafia?"

He nodded. "I didn't look for details— just enough to assure me that Hyannis was in very deep trouble. Then I packed up my equipment and my file and I came to Wimsy. To wait."

I chewed on that while he made the turn onto the Stone Road.

"Wait for what?"

"My dear idiot," he said, and I heard grim amusement in the light voice, "you do not go into debt with the Mafia to the tune of six hundred thousand dollars without receiving a call from Guido."

I thought of Craig and shivered abruptly.

"So you expected him to be hit— killed?"

He shook his head against the dark. "No. I expected that he would find his house had been broken into; that his car had been vandalized; that he himself had inexplicably acquired a sudden broken arm. I expected a warning, and when the warning came, I planned to hand my file over to Bill Jacques and blow Hyannis Stern's life into a million jagged pieces."

*Like he'd done to mine,* my inner ear added, though Fox did not.

I licked my lips. "Maybe he'd already had a warning."

"That seems likely."

We rode in silence for a while.

At the turn onto the Point Road, he spoke again, with a sort of quiet bitterness, "And I damn near got you killed." He looked over, and his face was bleak. "Say, 'thank you, Fox.'"

"I don't see that," I said. "Though you might have given your file to Scott's lawyer."

"I might have," he agreed. "And it might have established reasonable doubt. But it might not have done Scott as much good as you seem to think. Just because the Mob's after you doesn't mean you won't get killed by someone who thinks you shouldn't call his wife a whore in a public meeting."

"I see the problem," I admitted. "And if they let it be known they were looking at a connection to the Mafia, it might have spooked Craig..." I shook my head, creakily. "Man was a bomb, waiting to go off."

"It's hard to find good help nowadays," Fox agreed and slowed the truck. The tired scarlet letters on my mailbox blazed, caught in the glare of the headlights. "Here?"

"Here. Warning— dirt and gravel road."

"Four-wheel drive."

And good suspension. The truck's silk-smooth ride never faltered, all the way from the top of the drive to the dooryard. Fox pulled in close to the porch and killed the engine.

"Home sweet home," I said tritely, but I had to say something to lighten the sudden weight on my chest. God, it was good. Good to be home.

Fox slid out of the driver's seat. It took me a couple seconds to work the catch on the seatbelt and pop my door, by which time he was pulling my stuff from the seat behind me.

Carefully, ignoring the various aches and pains as well as I could, I turned in the soft leather seat and slid to the ground. My knees tried to buckle, but I wouldn't let them and stood there gripping the door frame while I chewed my lower lip to pulp.

"Are you all right?" Fox asked from beside me, and I let my eyes open to slits.

"Stiff. I'll be okay in a minute."

He nodded and stood there, apparently waiting for me to make good on my promise.

Teeth drilling lower lip, I took a chance and eased my grip on the frame. Okay. I moved my right leg, leaned my weight on it. It was shaky, but it would do.

"Okay," I said to Fox. "C'mon in."

The three steps up to the porch were a challenge. Fox stayed close behind me, which made it impossible to teeter backward, so I teetered forward instead and eventually made the door.

Twist the knob and she opened. Not locked. Naturally. I went inside, Fox at my heels.

Jasper jumped down from the kitchen table, raced over to me with his tail high and wove ecstatically around my legs. You would have thought I was his long-lost best friend.

"Where do you want this?" Fox asked, nodding at

the roll of plastic tucked under his arm.

"Lean it anywhere," I said and he leaned it against the wall behind the door, then walked over to the table and put down the plastic bag of odds and ends and the old umbrella.

Jasper made a noise like "Qwrrpt?" and dashed across just in time to neatly entangle Fox's legs as he turned.

"Hello," Fox said, disentangling himself without noticeable difficulty. He bent and held out a finger, which Jasper bumped with an enthusiastic nose. "Nice cat. What's her name?"

"His. Jasper." I yawned, belatedly getting a hand in front of it. "Excuse me."

"Nothing to excuse." Fox straightened and looked at me seriously. "You ought to go to bed, Jennifer. You look like hell."

"Compliments," I said, but he didn't smile. I held out my hand and he came forward to take it. "Thank you. For—for coming when I needed you."

"You're welcome," he said. "Is there anything you need? Aspirin? Groceries? You're at the east end of nowhere down here— do you have another car?"

"You going to run out and buy me one?" I asked and shook my head, carefully. "I'm fine. I've got buckets of aspirin and enough cat food to last Jasper a week. If I need anything else I can call Harry when I wake up, in about two days." Another yawn overtook me. "I'm really sorry."

"You're really tired. I'll get out of here so you can go to bed." He released my hand and went to the door, pulled it open.

"Fox." He looked back.

"It's not your fault," I said.

There was a slight pause before he inclined his head. "It's not my fault," he repeated expressionlessly and stepped out onto the porch. "Lock this," he said and pulled the door shut.

I locked the door, then went to the window and watched the green truck glide up the driveway.

After that, I fed and watered the cat— slow and painful work, that— then climbed the stairs, one curse at a time. In the bathroom, I downed the permitted three aspirin and pointedly ignored my reflection in the glass.

Jasper was already on the bed by the time I made my room. I kicked off my sneakers and climbed in with my clothes on.

Six hours later, the phone woke me up.

# 26

IT WAS JOHN THERRIAULT, good as his word, calling to let me know what he'd found out.

According to the Rhode Island State troopers, the problem with Craig's license was not that it was fake, but that it was all too real. However, the Craig Thomas Henderson it purported to identify was not the man Morris DuChamp had hired to boss his apple-picking crew. *That* Craig Thomas was also dead— and had been for three years.

The identity of Craig's so-called boss had not been established and John frankly didn't think that it ever would be. However, the gun— Craig's gun— was wanted by the FBI in connection with, "a couple other things, down south." In light of that, John was looking for some U.S. government help with getting a positive ID on Craig himself.

"M.E. says the cause of death was a broken neck, consistent with the car falling the way you said. 'Course, he was broke up pretty bad..." He let that drift off.

I said rather muzzily that I understood and a few minutes later, promising further news as it unfolded, John rang off. I managed to get the receiver cradled before I fell back to sleep.

The phone didn't ring again for another four hours. It was Merry, then, to say that Scott was sprung and the sheep were all accounted for.

I'd barely hung up from that conversation when Harry called, to give me hell for not calling her. "Leave a person to hear everything from the chickens," she groused. "How long's your car in the shop?"

"Forever," I said. "It's totaled. In fact, it's in pieces."

"Oh. Well, I'm sorry, Jen. I know how much you liked that car. Next time, though, be best to get a truck."

"Probably it would," I agreed.

"I'll be by later," Harry told me. "Bring you some soup and a few things."

"You don't have to go to all that trouble."

"It's no trouble," she said and hung up before I could argue the point.

Fully awake, I hit the reset and dialed a number. It rang twice before she picked it up.

"Hello?"

"Marian, it's Jen. I'm sorry I didn't call earlier. Wanted to let you know I'm okay."

"Fox called me around two. It's a good thing I've got my own line. My mother would have been furious." Marian sighed. "He said you were really tired and that you could hardly walk."

"Both true. Which is why I hadn't called. Fell into bed and just now woke up."

"That's all right." She hesitated, then blurted. "That's not going to be— permanent, is it, Jen?"

I blinked, backtracked and shook my head. It hurt. "No, it's not going to be permanent. Right now I'm one big bruise and it hurts to move *anything*. I'll be fine by— what's today?"

"Saturday."

"Then I'll be fine by Sunday night. I'm due at work." *No car,* my brain noted helpfully. *Have to call Bean's Taxi. Great.*

"How's the new modem?" I asked Marian.

"You never saw anything so fast," she said enthusiastically. "It's like flying."

I closed my eyes and swallowed. "Yeah? I'm going to be jealous." I hesitated. "Look, Marian..."

"I know. Fox said you'd probably sleep 'til Halloween. He said to leave you mail on the board, so you'd know I was worried." She paused. "I *was* worried, Jennifer."

"So was I," I told her. "But it came out all right. On average. I'll talk to you tomorrow, okay?"

"Okay. I hope you feel better soon."

"Me, too." We hung up.

I eased out from beneath the covers, went down to the bathroom and swallowed another three aspirin. In the hallway I hesitated, loath to try the stairs, disinclined to return to bed.

In the end, I limped back down the hall and pushed open the door to my room. I brought the computer up, used the mouse to choose the number and waited while the connection was made. The screen hesitated for a moment, then words began to appear:

**Welcome**
**You have reached**
**Random Access BBS...**

***

## About The Author

**Sharon Lee** was born in Baltimore, Maryland. Some time after that, she and her husband and oft-time co-author, Steve Miller, loaded up a rental truck and their fancy black go-fast car with all their worldly possessions, and, ably assisted by three intrepid and fearless cats, migrated to Maine.

Over the years, and in no particular order, Sharon has worked for several newspapers, been an administrative assistant at a university, an advertising copywriter, a sysop for several community bulletin boards, and the executive director of the Science Fiction and Fantasy Writers of America.

With Steve Miller, Sharon is the author of seven science fiction novels and over fifteen short works set in the Liaden Universe®, as well as a dozen single-authored short stories. *Barnburner* is her first mystery novel.

Sharon's interests include seashores, pine cone collecting, cats and cat whiskers, computers and, now that the era of the community BBS has ended, spends 'way too much time playing on the internet.

# About The Publisher

**SRM Publisher Ltd.** is an independent press specializing in publications for the Science Fiction, Fantasy, and Mystery communities. Our intent is to provide fiction and non-fiction of interest to readers and writers, librarians and collectors, fans and booksellers. We distribute directly, through the internet, at conventions, and whenever possible through the specialty booksellers who have been the hidden backbone of genre publishing for years.

A distant descendant of **BPLAN Virtuals** of Waterville, Maine as well as **General Avocations** and **Locust Run Press**, both of Owings Mills, Maryland, **SRM Publisher Ltd.** was formed in Winslow, Maine in 1995 to produce what was assumed to be a one shot publication of **Two Tales of Korval**— a chapbook consisting of several short stories of interest to readers of Sharon Lee and Steve Miller's Liaden Universe® series.

In short order one printing turned to two, three, and four and another chapbook was produced to meet the interest. With more than a dozen chapbook titles and thousands of copies of **Two Tales of Korval** in print both poetry and non-fiction were added to the chapbook mix and now— with **Barnburner**— SRM Publisher Ltd. has moved into trade paperbacks as well.

SRM Publisher Ltd.